Y0-ERO-493

The Bar X Golf Course

The

Written and Illustrated by Ross Santee

Bar X Golf Course

NORTHLAND PRESS / FLAGSTAFF

Copyright 1960 by Ross Santee
This 1971 edition published by
special permission of the Ross Santee Corral

ISBN 0–87358–085–0
Library of Congress Catalog Number 70–174996

• ALL RIGHTS RESERVED •

(1)

DAD JACKSON, owner of the Bar X Land and Cattle Company, has put in what we claim to be the biggest and sportiest golf courst in the world. This place is only a few miles off the main highway and Dad is catering to the tourist trade going to and from the coast.

With a million acres to work on Dad has put in a golf courst at the Bar X Ranch that will give any dude a real treat. It will give them all something to talk about after they have went back East.

At the Bar X Golf Courst a dude plays one hole a day. It takes nine days to go out and nine more to get back to the ranch or eighteen days in all. In this way Dad figgers that no matter how fond a dude is of the game by the time he has played the eighteen holes an' finished the courst he will have a belly full.

No. 2, the shortest hole, at Alkali, is not quite fifteen miles. We know this hole is short but Dad figgers the lack of distance is more than offset by the fact that No. 2 is up hill all of the way an' a dude must pack his own water. But No. 2 is the only hole on the courst where the dudes must make a dry camp.

Each dude is mounted, of course, at no extra cost to him an' each dude has a puncher to ride herd on him to see that he don't get lost.

There is only one thing about the courst that bothers us. I'll admit it has us stumped. Neither Dad nor us cow hands nor none of the dudes have been able to figger out what Par on the courst should be.

Ever since Dad put up the big sign down on the main highway the dudes have been stringing in. That sign is a thing that ketches every golfer's eye. It's certainly a pip.

THE BIGGEST AND SPORTIEST GOLF COURST
IN THE WORLD

RIDE A HORSE BETWEEN YOUR SHOTS

CAMP OUT UNDER THE STARS AT NIGHT

A COWPUNCHER RIDING HERD ON EVERY DUDE

18 GOOD ROUND-UP COOKS

Yes sir, that sign has done the trick. It was Dad's idea too. But the thing would probably have never come about except for the fact that two of Dad's cow hands, Balky Bill and the Cat Claw Kid by name, got a little drunker than somewhat at the Rodeo in Phoenix.

It was the usual trip that cow hands make after months out on the range. Balky and the Cat Claw Kid were grass bellied with spot cash. The Rodeo was something to look forward to as these two birds are good. The Cat Claw Kid can ride anything and Balky Bill is a roping fool. But as far as this particular Rodeo was concerned they didn't do so well.

The party began when Balky Bill and the Cat Claw Kid hit town. They stopped one night in Globe and bought a gallon of white mule. Next morning before they saddled up and headed down towards Phoenix way they had the jug refilled. Between this jug of liquid fire and ninety miles of desert heat neither Balky Bill nor the Cat Claw Kid could tell for sure whether they were mounted on a horse or traveling by air.

The Cat Claw Kid who promptly went to sleep behind the shutes could not be found when it came his turn to ride. He was disqualified. Balky Bill who always carries his liquor well was able to mount his horse when it comes his turn to rope. But as soon as his calf had left the shute an' headed on his way Balky bellered long and loud.

He insisted that at least ten head of calves had been turned out on him. Since only one calf had left the shute the judges stated in no uncertain terms that he was drunk an' seeing things or words to that effect. They disqualified him too. But the uproar woke the Cat Claw Kid. He didn't know what it was all about but as the affair showed promise of a fight he put in his twenty cents. The upshot of the whole thing was that both waddies left the Rodeo grounds feet first an' spent the night in jail.

Next morning when they paid their fines both punchers were released but instead of heading back for home they bought another jug. What happened then can only be surmised as neither waddie knew. But it was a week before they finally showed up at the ranch like two sheep killing dogs.

It was the night that Balky Bill and the Cat Claw Kid got back. The outfit was eating supper when Balky saw the car. It had just crossed Nine Mile Wash and was moving up Bean Belly Flat a headin' towards the ranch. At sight of it Balky and the Cat Claw Kid, both cagey birds, eased out the back door of the ranch house and headed for the brush.

The sheriff's car, of course, was what we all supposed it was. But instead there was a New York license on the car and two New York dudes got out.

Now every cowboy likes good clothes, he's fond of color too. But the garments these two dudes had on knocked the outfit for a loop. The caps, of course, were something we had seen before. But instead of pants which we supposed all grown men wore these birds were wearing rompers. And the color in their garments would put a squaw to shame. It dazed us so we couldn't speak. The outfit stood and stared. It wasn't until a dude spoke up an' asked if they were at the Cactus Country Club that we come out of it.

And that crack didn't go so well right in our own back yard. We thought these two strange fauna were making fun of us.

"No sir," says Dad, "this ain't no country club. You're at the Bar X Ranch."

Neither of the dudes looked any too comfortable right now as Dad Jackson looked as if he was undecided whether to shoot them hisself or just have them knocked in the head when Balky Bill and the Cat Claw Kid came out of the brush. They made it just in time. Both of them were laughing and the Cat Claw Kid explained.

It seems that he and Balky Bill had stole the sign just out of Phoenix when they passed the Country Club. And they had tacked it on the gate post where our road turns off the highway leading to the ranch.

This explained the whole business. For come to find out these two birds are golfers heading towards the coast a playing every golf courst that they find. Both dudes had a laugh

themselves. They took the joke all right. And they were for loading in their car an' heading back when Dad, who felt responsible for his cow hands' joke, insisted they stay to supper and spend the night with us.

I heard the cook whisper to Cat Claw that he would have made cream puffs for supper had he known that dudes were coming but neither dude throwed off any on the frijole beans and beef.

Both of them set in the stud game after supper and it was easy to see they'd looked at a hole card before. The game didn't run an hour until they had all the chips.

Yes sir, these dudes were good fellers in spite of their trick clothes. Their conversation was interesting too until they started talking golf. But mashies and brassies sounded like a kindergarten game. It was hard for us to imagine two grown men in rompers traveling from one golf courst to another just to hit a lousy golf ball — then hunt the dog-gone thing.

Balky Bill and I were leaving for Stray Horse next morning to range brand for a month. We had the mules all packed and were ready to pull out when the dudes got out their war clubs and made some practise shots. Never having seen this game Balky and I were curious to see how it was played.

From their talk it seems the dudes were way behind as far as their golf game went. They hadn't played since they left El Paso, that was the day before. It would be noon at least before they made it into Globe. And they could get in just one round. From what I gathered from their talk a man who plays just 18 holes of golf a day is loafing on the job.

The more I heard about the game the more curious I be-come. I thought the game had started when the tall dude took the longest club from his war bag and made several swipes at the air. But it was my mistake, he only took these practise swipes to get hisself warmed up. It wasn't until he finally set his ball up on the peg that the thing got serious. And it was easy to see from watching this dude that golf was far from simple.

After facing the ball a time or two the dude looked off down the flat with a far-away look in his eye. He's finding his range, thinks I. Then after a few more practise swipes he leaned over and stared at the ball.

I could tell that the dude meant business now. That far-away look was gone. He was working hisself into a lather and he intended to murder the ball. It was just when I thought he was ready that his feet began bothering him. He kept picking them up and putting them down like an old sore footed horse. I had finally decided he never would shoot when he wound up in a knot and let go.

Us cow hands were all looking down the flat at least a quarter away watching for dust to fly. We can't see a sign of the ball.

"Hot damn," yells Balky Bill, a slinging his hat. "He's knocked it plumb out of sight." But come to find out he's missed the whole works as the ball is still there on the peg.

He managed to hit it the next time but it didn't go very far. Fact is, none of the shooting by either dude was very impressive to me. I was willing to bet my saddle then that I could knock one further, once I learned that a man wasn't breaking any rules if he just stepped up an' hit it. For the little dude didn't mess around when it come his turn to shoot. He simply faced the ball and took a cut and he certainly connected.

Us cow hands were disappointed too at the length of the little dude's drive. Even when he caught one fair on the nose it was seldom over two hundred yards. Both dudes said two hundred yards was a good poke as they were both amateurs and later we all agreed that any one who could knock a golf ball further was a curly wolf at the game.

After watching the dudes both make a few licks I felt sure I could knock one a mile. But it wasn't until the dudes had struck a dozen blows a piece that they asked the rest of us to try it.

Dad struck the first blow for the outfit. He wasn't so keen to try. But he never missed a turn from then on. He didn't do so bad. He didn't get the ball in the air but it like to never quit rolling.

Balky Bill and the Cat Claw Kid shot next. Balky wasn't so good. But the Cat Claw Kid got holt of one and knocked it almost to the salt house. It wasn't hit where it was aimed but it was the longest ball by far. "A simple game," says Cat Claw, giving us a superior look.

The more I watched the game the easier it looked to me. But me being the shortest man in the outfit I didn't get to take a turn until the cook and horse wrangler shot. I'm pretty quick at ketching on to rules and things like that, I pegged this right away. As long as the tallest man shot first I'd never be the one to break a rule by shooting out of turn.

When it finally came my turn to shoot did I get holt of one? I could feel it clear down to my toes. I'll admit it wasn't where I was aiming for but even the Cat Claw Kid admitted it was a longer ball than his.

We took turn about all morning. The dudes had a peck of balls. As fast as we shot them up Balky and I loped down the flat an' picked them up again. We had our ponies an' the rest were all afoot. I kept thinking each time it came my turn I'd hit another one. But I found it wasn't so simple after all. My first shot was the only decent lick I made an' I didn't miss a turn all morning. At that I think I would have been all right if the tall dude had let me alone. As soon as I connected on my first lick he began to show me things.

First thing we knew it was dinner time. Balky and I cooked the meal as the cook had hurt his back so bad it was hard for him to move. It was a tough break too the way it come about. He was the only man in the outfit who hadn't made at least one decent lick. Somehow something or other always went cockeyed when Cookie went to shoot. At that I blame the tall dude for it as nobody could make a shot unless he put in his twenty cents. The accident occurred when the tall dude says that Cookie is hitting with his arms too much and tries to learn him how to pivot.

It took four of us to pack the cook into the ranch house as he lit right flat of his back. He's not so young no more like he onct was either. But suffering sisters an' fried horned toads! If he had only connected on that swing he would have knocked that ball a mile.

It was while we were eating dinner that the dudes suggested that we put in a couple of holes just like a regular golf courst. The place was ideal, they said. It looked as if Balky and I would miss the fun. But by the time we had finished dinner Dad said it was too late to start for Stray Horse and to turn the pack mules loose. But to keep our ponies saddled so's to use them shagging balls.

We wound up by putting in three holes. The two dudes planned the lay-out after making a lot of talk. The rest of us were rearing to go and were in a hurry to start.

The first hole started from the Ranch house just below the saddle rack and right by the big yucca on the flat we levelled off a little place and sunk a coffee can. The dudes said it was a Par 4 hole but since it was over four hundred yards and eight licks was the best anybody made it in we wanted to call it a Par 8. But the dudes said that wasn't according to Hoyle.

The second hole ran from the knoll by the calf pasture fence to the little flat topped butte acrost the canyon. "Sporty," the dudes called it but it was worse than that. It was only two hundred yards but if a man didn't make the butte in one lick he was a blowed up sucker. Once he got down in that canyon among the malapais and cactus he was lucky to get out in thirty licks an' not be bit by a snake.

The dudes called No. 2 a Par 3 but Par 30 was more like it as the tall dude was the only man to reach the butte on his drive and he made the doggondest lick I ever saw. No sir, I wouldn't have believed it if I hadn't seen it myself. When his ball stopped rolling it wasn't over three feet from where the coffee can was sunk. It looked like a two easy. "A birdie," says the tall dude.

There was a buzzard circling a dead critter down the flat a ways but that wasn't what he meant. Come to find out a birdie is a shot that's worth a dollar if it's made.

"Concede it," says the tall dude.

"Not on your life," says his pardner. "You'll put it down for me."

Both dudes had been playing for four bits a hole and a dollar on birdies so it looks like a dollar easy. But this tall dude is the nervousest man I've ever seen. Instead of just tapping the ball into the can he got down on all fours and took a squint like a kid at a game of marbles.

Then he picked up bits of sand. Two red ants frolicking near by were the next thing to ketch his eye. By the time he had herded the ants away I begun to get fidgety too.

When the dude finally faced the putt he had the same trouble with his feet as he did each time he drove and he had just got himself all set when Balky, who didn't know the rules of courst, asked Cat Claw for a match.

This upset the dude so much he got down and took another

Ross Santee

squint and removed more grains of sand. He went thru it all again. To watch him a man would swear his feet were sore as hell. But he finally got hisself tied in a knot. The putter come back slow. It was just as the blade come down again that Balky's pony nickered.

Well sir, I've seen horses jump when they were spooked but it was nothing to equal this. If the dude's hide hadn't been on real tight he would have jumped right out of it. What's more he was farther from the can on his third putt than he was when he started. But after making Balky and I lead our ponies away he finally got down in six.

The third hole was a Par 3 too. That wasn't so far off as it was only 140 yards. If a man could keep his ball in the air long enough to clear the big sand wash he wasn't apt to have much trouble.

We were all in the sand on No. 3 when another car drove in. Four Boston dudes heading to the coast had seen the sign and stopped. Dad explained the thing to them. These birds were golfers sure enough. It looked interesting to them. So Dad told them to get their war clubs out and try the courst themselves.

We played till dark and the short dude finally made the lay out in exactly thirty four. One of the Boston dudes shot a thirty six. Another a thirty seven. The best any of the outfit made was a sixty five. That was Cat Claw's score.

I finally won six dollars from Dad and the Cat Claw Kid. We didn't know the dudes were playing for money at first. When we learned they were playing for four bits a hole we played for four bits too so's not to break any rules.

I had a good chance to beat the short dude's score. It was the last round we played. I made the first two holes in fifteen by actual count. Cat Claw and Dad were counting too as after we began playing four bits a hole we counted each other's licks. By making the first two holes in fifteen it gave me nineteen licks to spare on No. 3. An' since I'd made an easy six on it the round before it looked pretty soft for me.

But something went wrong with my drive this time. The tall dude said I looked up. At any rate the ball lit in the middle of the big sand wash and I was there when it got dark.

After supper we cut the stud game out and practised putting at a knot hole on the bunk house floor at two bits a putt. One of the Boston dudes got hot and nearly broke the outfit.

The cook tried it a time or two but he had to quit because of his lame back. But he ordered a set of sticks from Buck an' Sears. Fact is, every man in the outfit ordered a set. Dad made the order out after supper.

(2)

THE DAY BALKY AND I moved up to Stray Horse it was too late to do any riding by the time we had killed a beef and shod a couple of horses. So we levelled off a little place in front of the tepee and sunk a coffee can.

When the two dudes left the ranch they gave the outfit the sack of practise balls and three or four old clubs to use until the ones we had ordered came from Buck an' Sears. So I slipped the putter and six balls into my bed roll the morning we left the ranch. Balky and I were putting for two bits a hole an' I'd just got into Balky for six bits when Scotty MacDonald rode up.

Scotty had seen our smoke from his place over on the river but Balky and I were so busy with our game we didn't see him until he was right into camp.

"Hoot, man," says Scotty when he sees what we are doing, an' then he says it again – "hoot."

Balky and I felt like two sheep killing dogs. Scotty is an old cow man an' we were afraid he wouldn't understand this dude game we were playing. But Scotty didn't notice either one of us. He was looking at the putter.

He finally got down off his horse a hootin' all the time an' onct he got the putter in his hands he started talking to hisself. It was the first time I ever seen Scotty excited. I figgered he'd been staying alone too much but after watching him tap a ball into the coffee can it was easy to see that he and the putter are not strangers.

I know Scotty's been living alone over on the river for the past thirty years. I was wondering where he learnt this dude game when Scotty tells us he played it as a boy in Scotland.

Come to find out this golf is not a new game after all. He says it was started years ago by some Scotch sheep herders. Of course, that's nothing to boost the game with a cowpuncher either. But Scotty says too his family has played the game for generations an' there has never been a sheep herder in his family. So I take it that the Scotch cowpunchers just naturally took it away from the sheep herders when they found it was a good game.

Scotty stayed all night an' left for his place next morning. When he left there was no doubt in our minds but what it was a Scotch game. Scotty talked more in that one evening than in all the fifteen years I've known him.

Balky and I had considerable trouble following some of his talk. For the "auld gutty ball" didn't mean a thing to us an' naturally we didn't know who "Auld Tom" or "young Tom Morris" was an' neither one of us ever heard of Andra Kirkaldy. But from what Scotty said they were all curly wolves when it come to this game of golf.

Scotty always rode with us a part of the time when we were branding on Stray Horse as a few of his cows run there.

But we didn't see him again for a week. Balky and I were just fixing to ride over and see if anything was wrong when he rode into camp again an' it was Balky and I who got het up this time. Scotty was packing three new golf clubs in his Winchester scabbard he had made all by hisself.

We got out the practise balls an' it looked like a different game when Scotty played it. He could just naturally make a golf ball play dead an' roll over.

He finally let Balky and I try the new clubs. After each one of us had made two licks a piece an' each one of us had lost two balls Scotty said we had better stick to putting. Scotty could have broke Balky an' I if he had been a mind to. But he said two bits a hole was too much an' he wouldn't shoot for over a nickel.

I told Scotty the rules called for two bits a putt just the same as a hole must be played for four bits and a dollar on birdies. But Scotty said there was nothing in the rules about it so I guess he ought to know. But at that I guess it was just as well we played for a nickel. It made it light on me an' Balky Bill as we putted for five hours an' never won a hole.

Balky and I lost eight dollars to Scotty between us by the time we were ready to move back to the ranch. I figgered it was worth it as Scotty gave Balky and I lessons every evening an' I figgered we would be plenty tough for the boys when we got back to the ranch.

We left Scotty the two practise balls. We wanted to leave the putter as the clubs we ordered from Buck an' Sears should be at the ranch. But Scotty wouldn't take the putter. He liked his wooden one.

It was late when Balky and I got back to the ranch as we had some trouble with the pack mules. There was one jack that that should have been worked over with a niblick. It put us in late for supper as the hands were already in the bunk house putting at that knot hole on the floor. Balky an' I didn't take time to cook a warm bait. We gathered some cold steak an' hurried to the bunk house an' the game like to wound up in a fight.

It seems the cook had went to Phoenix to have a chiropractor work on his back which he hurt when the tall dude tried to learn him how to pivot. While he was in Phoenix he went out to see Walter Hagen play golf. An' Balky an' I can't make a move but what the cook tells us we are wrong. We don't stand like Hagen. We don't tap the ball like Hagen. In fact, nothing we do is like Hagen.

Balky an' I were doing pretty well as it was. We didn't say anything until we got back the eight dollars we lost to Scotty MacDonald but finally after he had missed a couple of easy putts for a win Balky says – "who is this guy Hagen anyway?" The cook says he's a prize golfer an' he showed us his picture in the paper to prove it.

That settled it for the outfit but it didn't for Balky Bill for he asked the cook did he ever hear of Andra Kirkaldy? And the cook says No.

"Well, he's a prize golfer from Scotland who invented this game," says Balky, "an' he don't putt that way."

I was afraid Balky would spill the beans about us taking lessons from Scotty MacDonald. Balky was getting hot under the collar and he and I were going to play the cook and the horse wrangler next day for four bits a hole. But the cook went to his bunk without any more talk an' the game broke up right away. But the cook an' the horse wrangler were no set-ups like Balky and I expected.

We divided up all the balls in the outfit before we started an' it gave us eight balls a piece. I was afraid we would run short but the outfit had lost most of the balls the dudes left while Balky an' I were away an' eight a piece was the best we could do.

The cook couldn't take a full swing because of his back but he was right down the middle. The horse wrangler was wild as a hawk but how he could lam that old ball.

The horse wrangler, being the tallest one, shot first. Balky an' the cook got in an argument right there. The cook insisted he was taller than Balky. I said Balky was the tallest and the horse wrangler was neutral. But the cook wouldn't take my word for it an' while they went back to the ranch house to let Dad measure them I broke my new driver from Buck an' Sears in making a practise lick. That was my first

bad break as neither the cook nor the horse wrangler would let me use theirs for fear it would happen again. Balky finally let me use his driver but he was pretty well spooked hisself an' kept telling me to ease up on my swing an' not take such a cut at the ball until he finally got me clear off my game before we even got started.

Dad finally decided in favor of the cook so Balky an' I shot last. And the horse wrangler stepped up an' lammed one down the flat for a good two hundred yards. When the cook topped his and didn't get over fifty yards I felt better as Balky did pretty well on his first lick. But Balky was so afraid I'd break his new driver he finally talked me out of my first lick and I got no further than the cook.

On my second shot I tried to think of some of the things Scotty had showed me. But I got to thinking about too many things at onct as I got off in the toolies an' before I could get back on the flat again I had lost a couple of balls.

I figgered we had lost the hole so I rode over to see how the horse wrangler was coming an' come to find out he had been having hard luck too as he had lost four balls already an' he wasn't out of the cat claw thicket yet.

The cook was still in sight going right down the middle. But as he was walking an' leading his horse I knew he wasn't hitting them very far. Balky Bill was nowhere in sight.

I finally found Balky up a side canyon an' he wasn't doing so bad as he had only lost one ball. As I was riding back to start play again I saw the horse wrangler lope up to where the cook was playing a time or two an' then ride back into the brush.

The last time he rode up I could see the cook waving his arms as if he was lathered about something. And the wrangler didn't ride into the brush any more. He just set there on his horse. Balky finally come in sight. But the cook an' the horse wrangler had been waiting at the coffee can a good hour before Balky and I got to the place.

It didn't take a man with more than half an eye to see that there had been trouble between the cook and the horse wrangler. Both of them were swelled up like two poisoned pups an' neither one was speaking.

Come to find out the wrangler had lost all his balls and all of the cook's except the one the cook was playing. The wrangler was on the prod because the cook wouldn't give him the ball so he could finish the hole. And the cook was red-eyed because the wrangler had lost all the balls.

Then we got into an argument as to who won the hole. The cook made it in thirty-two licks. I had a sixty-four an' Balky a fifty-two so the cook claimed they won it. But the horse wrangler admitted he had took eighty-three before he lost his last ball and he wasn't even out of the brush yet. So Balky and I claimed the hole as the wrangler didn't even finish as we won't give him any more balls.

We weren't getting any place about it until Dad rode up to tell us dinner was ready. When we put it up to him he said the best way he knew was to call the bets off and play the hole over again after dinner.

We changed horses and divided the balls again after dinner. The cook had one left, Balky Bill had two and I had five. It gave us two balls a piece and we made a new rule that as soon as a man lost two balls he couldn't borrow from any one else.

It looked like trouble between the cook and the horse wrangler when we started as the cook put on his six shooter. When he saw this the wrangler went an' got his 30-30. Balky and I didn't intend to get caught flat-footed in case of a fight so we went an' got our guns too. But we weren't even half started on the first hole until we had lost all the balls.

A man can't play this game with a lot of things on his mind and even the cook who was right down the middle all morning was having trouble with his shots too.

After we lost all the balls we went over to No. 2 and hunted in that canyon where us an' the dudes had been playing the first day an' we finally found twelve balls.

It gave us three a piece again but no one remembered how many licks they had taken so we started the hole over again.

Balky and I should have won it as the cook and horse wrangler were out of balls again on their fourth licks while Balky and I still had one ball a piece. An' neither one of us were over one hundred yards from where the coffee can was sunk when it got dark and we couldn't find the can. By the time we got the can located Balky and I each lost our ball. So we called the bets off again and went back to the ranch house.

But Balky and I would have took those birds easy if it hadn't got dark.

Dad made two rules when we got in. The first one was that nobody can pack a gun on the golf courst and the second one was there was to be no playing except when we got in of evenings and on Sundays. Dad says too, in case none of us knew it, that the Bar X outfit was still in the cow business.

(3)

IT WAS SHORTLY AFTER Balky an' I got back from Stray Horse that Swede gave me this dog. I figgered a houn' would come in handy when it came to hunting balls. Several punchers now have dogs that are trained to retrieve lost balls. But of all the dogs in the outfit there are none in Top Flite's class. If I do say so myself he is a most unusual dog. I probably never would have come by the dog except for the fact that he was misunderstood. The Swede who knows his houns as well as any man slipped up in Top Flite's case.

A small boy and a houn' pup in many respects are very much alike. The boy will follow a rabbit's track and pretend he is hunting a bear. It is always the unusual boy who doesn't fool hisself. He knows the track is only a rabbit track and can never be anything else.

The other pups in Top Flite's litter all showed promise of becoming varmint dogs as soon as they could walk — by trailing the red ants about the camp and bawling on their tracks. But Top Flite never went in for puppy games like that. A red ant was just a ant to him. He didn't fool hisself. Swede thought the pup was simply dumb. That was Swede's big mistake. He didn't realize that Top Flite was the unusual case. And that even as a pup the dog had visions of hunting better things.

It usually depends on how much training he gets as to how much a dog is worth. But with all the training in the world some dogs just go so far. Often in talking about our golf houns at night around the fire we discuss my pooch's case and the punchers are all agreed that all the training in the world couldn't make him what he is. Top Flite had something that sets him apart from all the other dogs and by this I don't mean that my dog has any bigger fleas.

Any of the other golf houns will find a ball no matter what its make. But if it happens to be a cheap ball my dog will have none of it. He will smell out a Hagen or a Dunlap any time, no matter how thick the brush. He has never overlooked a Top Flight yet. That's how he came by his name.

He was always a very sensitive dog and I'll admit as a pup he sometimes made a slip. It was really pitiful to watch the dog after he had pulled a boner. When he brought me in a Kroflite or a Silver King my dog was overjoyed. But if by chance he made a slip and brought me in a cheap ball he would hide his head in shame. Top Flite was so ashamed that he refused to eat for two days onct after bringing me a Whippet.

It was shortly after Balky Bill and I had played the horse wrangler and the cook that I came by this pooch. Having lost all the golf balls that we had the outfit went back to poker. But the stud game was pretty flat to every one after playing this game of golf. We decided to see if we couldn't find at least one ball to putt with and the whole outfit was combing the brush on No. 1 when Swede Larsen rode in with his dogs.

The Swede is a government hunter who makes his living by hunting mountain lion and bear. When he rode up and saw the outfit combing the brush he thought we were tracking a varmit. When he found what we were hunting the Swede was so disgusted that he rode into the ranch and unsaddled without a word to us.

But Swede hadn't talked to anyone in two months' time. He wanted conversation. There was no one left at the ranch house – even the cook had gone. Swede stuck it out for a little while then he came back out where we were hunting on No. 1.

The Swede has an eye like an Apache. He hadn't been there five minutes before he picked up a ball. When they saw what Swede had found his houns all went to hunting too an' in less than fifteen minutes they had brought in twenty balls.

We wanted Swede to take his houns over in the canyon on No. 2 but he was afraid of spoiling his dogs. Swede was afraid if the game affected a dog as it did a man onct his dogs had really got a taste of it they were apt to quit a bear or lion track and go to hunting golf balls. It was then Swede told me of this pup he owned. That was how Top Flite came.

It was evident Swede didn't think much of the game of golf from little digs he made. All through supper he made remarks that could pass as dirty cracks about the bags of golf sticks that stood in every corner of the ranch house. When we began putting at the knot hole on the bunk house floor he would have none of it.

But cowboys are a funny breed. Take any game where a man just uses his feet and hands an' a puncher is apt to be good. It is only when a game becomes complicated and requires a little use of the head that a puncher loses interest. While Swede is a government hunter now he is still a cow-puncher at heart. Onct he took the putter in his hands an' tried it onct we knew that Swede was hooked.

Dad kept neglecting to take down the sign that Balky and Cat Claw stole. There was hardly a day went by but what a carload of dudes drove in. Often as many as four cars a day came rolling into the ranch. All of them stayed over an' took a shot at the courst. There was one dude from f.o.b. Detroit who came alone and stayed at the ranch two weeks.

After Dad made his ruling that we could only play on Sundays and of evenings when we got in it was pretty tough on us as a man can't play this game if he plays one day a week. We found that golf is a game that should be played every day. It is a game that should take all a man's time if he is to play it well. The outfit always started a round each evening when we got in. But on weekdays it was always dark before we could finish a hole.

The cook, of courst, played every day. The cook in any cow outfit is always an exception. Even Dad who owned the outfit couldn't shoot him any pills. After breakfast just as soon as he put on a pot of beans an' got his pony saddled he would grab his clubs an' start. An' his golf game didn't help his cooking none as far as we could see.

At noon when we got in the beef would be half cooked an' the biscuits were always burned. After he put in all his time on the courst the bean pot was always dry. Time was when he at least made a stab at sorting the gravel from the frijoles but not after he took up golf. There wasn't a man in the outfit — excepting Dad who wore store teeth — who didn't crack at least one tooth on the gravel in the beans.

Cookie still wore a flour sack as an apron, the badge of all round-up cooks. But instead of overalls he wore rompers now he had sent from Buck an' Sears. Cowpunchers are usually a long suffering breed when it comes to the chuck they get and Cookie was pretty bad. But it wasn't the cooking that burned us up. It was the way the cook's game improved.

None of us could play him now unless he gave us strokes. After our Sunday round of golf Cookie had all the chips. He could give out strokes to every man until it looked like a pretty good bet. But when the round was over we all knew the strokes that Cookie had given us weren't half enough.

Cookie and the dude from f.o.b. Detroit played together every day. It was pretty soft for the dude. As fast as Cookie won our dough the dude from f.o.b. Detroit took it off'n the cook. It was just as well that the dude from f.o.b. Detroit only stayed at the ranch two weeks. When he said that only business took him on to the coast we knew he meant it too. An' we knew the proposition was a good one or he couldn't have afforded to leave.

Onct the dude from f.o.b. Detroit had gone the cook had it all his way. It was bad enough to lose to him. But a man couldn't even take a practise lick until Cookie was right on tap to tell him he was wrong. It was Hagen this and Hagen that, every move we made. If Hagen had drove into the ranch about that time I would have took a shot at him myself. No sir, Hagen's life wouldn't have been worth a dime. The outfit was fed up. When the dude from f.o.b. Detroit sent Cookie Jones' book then Cookie switched to Jones.

It seems this Bobby Jones was a prize golfer too an' a curly wolf at the game. I liked his book myself. For it seemed that according to this book of Jones' even the cook was wrong. The book sounded simple too an' made golf an easy game. I had just got far enough with Jones that sometimes I could grip a club like him when the dude from f.o.b. Detroit sent Cookie Alex Morrison's book an' we found we were wrong again.

According to Morrison the Vardon or overlapping grip was out — a man should interlock. No one could properly cock his wrist an' pull the trigger unless he gripped that way. It sounded simple too. But the thing that caught Cookie's eye about Morrison's book was this secret about the chin.

Cookie said as long as a man's chin was pointed back of the ball a man could make no mistakes. He could shut his eyes an' shoot. Keeping an eye on the ball was all boloney now, it wasn't necessary. By pointing the chin just back of the ball there couldn't be any tension. Cookie even went so far as to say that if a man's chin was pointed properly the shot became automatic.

And Cookie practised what he preached. I'll give him credit for that. He practised all the time. The fact that the dude from f.o.b. Detroit was gone and Cookie was alone on the courst didn't bother that hombre any. Each morning after breakfast he would saddle his horse an' start. Often when we got in at night Cookie was still at work on the flat with a sack of practise balls an' his book in front of him.

Even when washing the pots an' pans he practised pointing his chin. He could point it back of anything an' do it mighty quick. No matter what he was doing now his head was always cocked. When eating he would eye a bean on his plate from the corner of his eye much like an old rooster eyes a grain of corn before he picks it up. Any one not knowing the cook would have swore his neck was stiff.

He quoted Morrison so much the outfit fell for it. If one of us doubted anything he had the book to prove it. Some of the hands said it helped their roping when they were out on the range. Balky Bill was strong for it. He claimed it was the secret of roping too. If a man's chin was only pointed properly he couldn't miss a throw.

One day when Balky and I were out on the range we jumped a maverick cow. Balky didn't get a smear because of the brush but I missed an easy throw. I couldn't understand it at first until Balky put me right. He said the only reason I missed was the fact that I didn't point my chin.

An' Cookie's game improved all right. There was no doubt in the least as to that. But somehow he never could reach the place where the shot became automatic. Cookie still topped a ball occasionally an' he'd pop one in the air. Once in a while he would up an' miss the ball completely although it wasn't as common with him as it was with the rest of us. But Cookie never blamed the book just because he missed a shot. He still insisted like Morrison that the proper pointing of the chin was the secret of all good golf.

For Cookie had one fault he couldn't overcome. He told me so hisself an' there were tears in Cookie's eyes when he spoke to me about it. He could point his chin as well as any man until he went to shoot. But all of the practice in the world couldn't make him keep it pointed.

But in spite of this fault that Cookie had he was too good for any of us. No matter how many strokes we got it was never enough. He won enough on weekends to buy a set of matched clubs. He even got to the place where he could knock over a dude occasionally when a car drove into the ranch.

We had just decided to frame him. The outfit was all agreed. I was to bring Scotty MacDonald down to play the cook when Dad sprung the idea of putting in a real golf courst an' everything else was off.

(4)

DAD JACKSON always began his thinking where his cow hands had left off. Dad started as a cowboy too like all the rest of us. But instead of using just his feet an' hands he used his head as well. It was this particular trick that set Dad apart from the rest of us an' made him what he was.

There was nothing small about Dad either, not even his hands an' feet. It was natural when he decided to put in a golf courst at the Bar X Ranch that he would do it big. As usual with everything he did Dad worked it out an' planned the thing before he called us in.

"I admit," says Dad, "that some of the fine points about this game are still hazy to me in spite of all I've seen. But at least I have a working knowledge of the game after talking to the dudes. From what I gather from their talk it's a popular game back East. Most every one you see back there packs golf sticks with them every place they go.

"Now this ranch is only a few miles off the main highway. Some days there are as many as a hundred cars that pass this place going to an' from the coast. I figger that these same people who play this game back East are these tourists who pass the ranch. It was the sign that Balky an' Cat Claw stole that gave me this hunch of mine. Since it's been up down on the main highway there hasn't been a day but at

least one carload of dudes have drove in here to play a round of golf.

"Now I've watched these dudes all pretty clost an' from what I've observed right here at the ranch the tougher you make it for a dude an' the more miserable he is while he's out on the courst the better he likes this game.

"We've got a million acres to work on an' I aim to do it big. Keep the thing big, you understand, an' give the dudes a real treat. Give them all something to talk about after they have went back home. I'm not fixing to put in no little courst like a dude can play in the East. On our courst we wont have any dinky Par 3 holes. We'll call our shortest hole a Par 300 an' let it go at that.

"The way I've worked it out the dudes will play one hole a day. It will take a dude nine days to go out an' nine more to get back to the ranch. In this way no matter how fond a dude is of the game by the time he has played the eighteen holes he will have a bellyful.

"I'm taking down the sign that Balky an' Cat Claw stole

an' I'm putting up a real sign in its place where all who pass may see an' the dudes will know what's in store for them when they play golf at this ranch.

"The way I've planned the lay-out the first hole will start at the ranch house. The green will be at Sweet Water just a little better than twenty miles from the ranch. If a dude keeps to the flats where he belongs No. 1 is an easy hole. There is one cut off on the hole where a dude could save a few miles. The cut off means trouble sure but if any dude wants to try it it is his own affair, of courst. I figger it is better to give the dudes an easy hole when they start out from the ranch as most of them wont be used to riding an' are apt to be pretty soft.

"No. 2 — the shortest hole on the courst — is not quite fifteen miles. I know this hole is short but I figger the lack of distance is more than offset by the fact that this hole is uphill all of the way an' a dude must pack his own water. No dude will be allowed to start the hole without a full canteen. While this hole is short it is a hole where a dude will find plenty of hazards. As you cow hands know, it is nothing but a ridge or hog back all of the way covered with buck brush an' cactus.

"Where Black Canyon cuts in about ten miles up is what really makes it sporty. By carrying the canyon on his shot a dude can cut off at least two miles.

"While No. 3 is a longer hole it's nothing but a breather. The dudes will shoot from the top of that big flat rock. The green is at Sycamore. On this hole a dude will get plenty of distance on his shots as it's down hill all the way. Even if a dude tops his ball off No. 3 tee it should roll at least a mile.

"The fourth green is on Deer Creek, just below the big steer trap. The way this creek winds an' twists about a dude will find plenty of hazards. A wood can be used at certain times but any dude to finish the hole will have to know his niblick.

"No. 5 is another breather again where a dude will keep to the flats. You will find the green below the first salt ground. This is really an easy hole. Any dude who can make long brassie shots should eat his supper early.

"At No. 6 you will find the green at Stinking Springs. It wont be much of a camp but it's the only water in those parts an' we can't do any better.

"On No. 7 the green is located just back of Tin Cup Springs. I know it's rough in there an' I've put the green on No. 8 below the wire trap on Stray Horse. Both of these holes are a little rough but you will find good water there.

"The ninth hole is at Devil's Gap an' while it's not a long affair any dude will know he has played some golf if he can finish it in a day.

"The tee shot from Round-up butte calls for a carry acrost the Gap. On this shot it will be up to the dude, his conscience can be his guide. The carry in the shortest place isn't over fifty yards. But the more distance a dude bites off on his carry the more distance he can save. A dude who can keep his ball in the air for a carry of a hundred and fifty yards can save at least six miles. Now that's the first nine holes as I see it although we may have to make some changes later.

"I've tried to make it easy on the dudes on the first nine holes they play as most of them will be soft. But by the time he has been out nine days an' played the first nine holes they should be ready for some golf. The second nine as I've worked it out, is really a sporty affair. While the mileage is no longer any dude who plays the second nine will know he's been somewhere.

"The 18th hole coming into the ranch is the only one that's down hill all the way. I figger it will look better to any waiting customers at the ranch to see a dude finish strong. But as far as the other eight holes go there's not a breather among them.

"No. 10 will parallel Devil's Canyon all of the way. If a dude can keep down the middle he can use a wood on almost every poke. A hook will cause a man no trouble either. It's really a slugger's hole. But God help any dude who slices on this hole! He's simply out of luck. An' No. 11 as I've worked it out will follow the canyon back.

"No. 12 is our first river hole. It's really a little rough. You will find the green on that flat topped butte, the one just below Squaw Peak. But of all the holes as I see them I like the 13th best. Here the dudes will shoot from Squaw Peak an' as you boys know it's all of an hour's climb.

"A dude can't top his tee shot here or it's just too bad for him but an ordinary shot will carry the river below. When the river is a little high it will be some trouble to cross. So shoot your dudes over on that old mine cable if they are afraid to swim their horses.

"The 14th green is at Horse Shoe bend. An' you'll have no trouble locating the 15th as it's on the flat below Scotty MacDonald's place. The 16th green is at Sentinel. You may have some trouble on the 17th hole as it crosses the river again. But the 17th green is at Golden Roll, the last of the river holes. An' I figger no matter whether a dude is afraid of water or not he will take a chance of swimming his horse as it's the only way back to the ranch."

The morning after Dad gave us the lay-out six pack outfits left the ranch. Each outfit had its orders to put in three of the greens. Our outfit put in the first green at Sweet Water where the dudes were to camp the first night. Balky Bill, the Cat Claw Kid an' I put in this green an' we made a good job of it.

After we levelled off the place we put down this stuff Dad brought from Phoenix in the truck. Some sort of composition, Dad said it was, that was made from cotton seed hulls. Dad would really have liked to put in grass greens but grass wasn't practical because of the shortage of water. An' besides Dad couldn't afford to keep a cow hand at each green to herd the stock away.

But the first green certainly looked pretty when we sunk the can in the middle of her an' put up flag No. 1. Except for a few boulders an' rocks that were too big to move it was as level as a floor.

We put the next green in at Alkali, about fifteen miles east of there. I didn't think much of No. 2 as I never liked a dry camp but the third hole at Sycamore more than made up for it.

Sycamore has always been one of the outfit's best camps because of its water and trees. It was a mighty smart move on Dad's part to put No. 3 there as he knew the dudes would all be needing water when they finished No. 2.

It took us two weeks to put in our three holes an' the night that we got back to the ranch I thought I was seeing things. There must have been twenty cars parked in front of the house an' there were dudes of every size an' shape a milling round, all of them in rompers.

Dad had fixed up a runt courst in the calf corral for the women an' kids to play while their dudes were out on the courst. But all the dudes had taken to the runt courst too. There were more people playing in the calf corral than there had been calves in the place in a month.

When we unsaddled an' went in to eat there were three flunkies helping the cook. He was swelled up like a poisoned pup because of the extra work.

Dad had put up some cabins while we were gone an' they looked mighty neat. Each one was a setting off by itself half hid by the pepper trees.

The rest of the punchers had beat us in an' when Dad learned that all of the greens were finished he announced to all an' sundry that the courst would be open next day. That night when the dudes were bedded Dad came out to the bunk house to give us hands a talk.

"This thing," he says, "is new to all of us. A lot will be up to you. For wrangling dudes on a golf courst will be different from working stock. Each dude will have a puncher to ride herd on him an' I expect you to stick to your dudes. I aint askin' none of you to pack any sticks. Each dude will carry his bag of sticks on his saddle horn which will make it handy for him.

"You will find the camp all ready with a cook an' horse wrangler waiting at Sweet Water when you get in tomorrow night. You will find this same arrangement at every other camp.

"Now, I've given this thing a lot of thought an' the biggest problem as I see it will be losing the dudes on the courst. I know it's bound to happen at times as brushy as some of it is. But if a dude should get lost an' starve to death they might hold me responsible for it. An' we can't afford to have sixteen punchers off at one time an' play held up just to hunt for one lost dude.

"Now, one thing more an' get this straight. It's the last thing I have to say. I don't want any dude coming back to the ranch just because he's tired after playing a couple of holes. I'm not telling any of you to use your guns but be sure to pack 'em along. For unless he has played the eighteen holes an' finished the courst I don't want any dude coming back to the ranch unless he has busted a leg."

The formal opening of the courst next morning was a big success in spite of some trifling things. When we started each puncher was lined up on the flat long side of the dude he was herding. There were sixteen dudes an' sixteen cow hands all mounted on good cow ponies. Dad was smiling all over an' since he wanted the dudes to feel as much at home as possible Dad wore a pair of rompers.

"Gentlemen," said Dad, "speaking for myself an' my cow hands, we are honored by your company at this little dedication of what I claim an' knows to be the biggest golf courst in the world. Gentlemen, I hope ———."

Dad's speech was cut a little short. He had considerable more to say but just then this fat dude I'm herding accidentally poked a golf stick in his pony's flank an' instead of the opening Dad had planned it began to look like a Rodeo. When my fat dude's pony began to buck several of the other ponies come unwound an' in less time than it takes to tell it at least half of our dudes were unhorsed.

Of courst, the ponies shed their dudes the first real jump they made. Since that was done so easy they tried to unload

the golf bags. The bags were tied to the saddle horn, it was hard to buck them loose. But there were golf sticks an' dudes scattered all over the flat before we caught all the ponies.

Some of the dudes were a little upset by this incident. My fat dude was pretty well spooked. He was for playing afoot from then on. It wasn't until I promised to pack his golf sticks for him that he would get back onto his horse. One dude's wife who was watching the start rounded up her dude an' herded him to the house. She refused to let him go. An' the way that woman talked to Dad would put a mule skinner to shame.

Dad had let the dudes draw numbers to see who made the first shot on the courst. This honor fell to my fat dude's friend, Wicker Bill was herding him. An' Dad had planned to shoot his six shooter as a signal for each dude to start. But he had to give the idea up after firing one measly shot. These dudes were as spooky of a pistol as a wild horse just off the range.

There was a little delay while Wicker's dude selected a certain pet wood of his. Dad stood just behind the dude an' give him plenty of time. It was just as the dude wound up for his swing that Dad pulled his six shooter off an' hollered to let her go!

I've seen plenty of gun shy men in my time but Wicker's dude was the worst. It upset him so he couldn't even hit his ball an' he passed up the honor of making the first shot.

A dude who said he was from Chicago volunteered to start her off. He said the shooting wouldn't bother him. But when Dad saw how it was upsetting all the other dudes he cut the shooting out. But this Chicago dude didn't do so well in spite of all his talk.

He missed the ball completely his first lick. Then he popped one into the air. Fact is, none of the shooting by the dudes was very impressive to me except a lick that one tall dude made. He certainly got holt of one an' when Cat Claw who was herding him rode off he was smiling from ear to ear. Cat Claw knew if every lick was half that far he would be eating supper early.

All of the dudes finally took their licks an' began to string off down the flat. My fat dude an' Wicker's come last. When both dudes rolled their tee shots off not half as far as they could throw the thing I thought they were in for a walk. But after we got strung out a piece they both did pretty well. Sometimes riding for most two hundred yards before they dismounted to shoot.

They didn't hit 'em very far an' except for a slice that my dude had they both kept pretty straight. It wasn't long before we began overtaking an' passing dudes who had started ahead of us.

As long as we kept to the flats we found the balls all right. There wasn't enough grass in the country to even hide a golf ball. When the country roughened up a bit Wicker an' I rode on ahead an' spotted the balls each time our dudes would shoot. Both dudes were using Whippets an' Top Flite wouldn't work.

My fat dude was a friendly dude an' very fond of dogs. He couldn't understand why Top Flite growled at him when he tried to pet the dog. I finally told the dude just how Top Flite felt but he didn't believe the yarn. Not having any good balls in his bag I couldn't prove it to him.

We had played about six miles, I guess, an' we hadn't lost many balls, not over a dozen a piece I'd say. We had passed all the dudes who had started ahead of us except the one Cat Claw was herding an' Wicker an' I were just speaking of him, wondering if he wasn't already in camp on No. 1 when we saw Cat Claw coming back our way riding at a lope.

It seems this long hitting dude of his was out of balls an' he has already lost a peck. Cat Claw said he hit 'em so dog-goned far there was no chance of finding them. An' besides he had tried to cut through the hills when he learned that way was shorter. But our dudes were afraid of running short themselves. They wouldn't part with any balls. I offered to let Cat Claw take Top Flite back with him. Cat Claw said his dude was using Whippets too so it wasn't any use. There was nothing for Cat Claw to do but go back to the ranch for some balls. So he headed his pony for the ranch. The last we saw of him he was riding at a lope.

It wasn't until we were out about ten miles that our dudes began to slow up. My fat dude was having it pretty tough. He wasn't used to riding an' right here was where I found that all my previous ideas concerning dudes were wrong. This dude of mine was wet with sweat. I'll bet he shed ten pounds. But do I hear a cheep from him? I'll tell a man I don't an' it surprises me still more when he says he's from N. Y.

We finally came to a water hole an' watered our dudes out. It only took a little rest till they came alive again. When we told them they only had four more miles to go you should have seen those birds perk up. Once we came in sight of the green an' they could see the flag they finished like two tired old cow ponies when they come in sight of the ranch.

The cook an' horse wrangler were waiting there to watch our two dudes finish. So was Old Dolphadios, the Mexican salt packer, who had just got in with a load of balls for the dudes an' a bunch of extra clubs. After our dudes tapped their balls into the can we shook hands all around.

An' right there was where the new cook on No. 1 come

through an' proved that he was regular. He dug a bottle out of the brush an' we drank to the health of our dudes. Of all the dudes who had started they were the first to finish the hole.

(5)

IT WAS AN HOUR after we finished before the other dudes began to string in. All of us had eaten an' were waiting at the green. Sometimes a single would come in, then three or four in a bunch but half of the dudes were still out on the courst when it got too dark to see. All of them came in at dark except Cat Claw and his dude. When they hadn't got in at bed time we figgered his dude was lost.

Some of the dudes didn't feel any too well when they got into camp. Nine of them by actual count were walking and leading their horses. Some of the dudes had tried to cut off when they found it would save a few miles. Every dude who had tried it was completely out of balls.

The dudes had made a jack pot just before they left the ranch. Originally there were sixteen in the pot until this woman gathered her dude an' took him back to the house. Each dude had put up a dollar on each hole. The jack pot was to go to the dude who was the first one in each night. It was really my dude's money as he was the first to hole out. But he split the pot with his pardner as they were playing together.

Some of the dudes didn't take it so well when it came to paying bets. There were bets on how many licks they took as well as who would finish first. Two dudes from Pittsburgh, Pa. were having it up and down. They had a bet between them as to how many licks they would take.

The punchers who were herding them were supposed to tally the strokes. A right smart job at best. To complicate matters further neither of these waddies could have counted to a thousand off hand if his life hung on the deal. They had bawled the count all up until it was quite a mess. There was a difference of some hundred odd strokes they couldn't agree upon.

One of the cow hands, not wanting to tip his hand to the fact that his entire schooling had consisted of learning to follow a cow through the brush, at least had a good idea. This waddie picked up a pebble each time his dude made a shot. He figgered that the dudes could count the rocks themselves

when they got in an' leave him out of any argument. This puncher's idea was really good as far as it went. It worked for several miles. But this waddie finally had to unload an' throw his rocks away when his pony began to play out.

Most of the dudes felt better after they downed their evening bait. The cook on No. 1 had done hisself proud on the meal he had slung together. The dudes tore into the beef an' frijole beans like a pack of hungry coyotes. But the two dudes who caught my eye as I watched them feed were two dudes from Boston. Living in cow camp as I have I've seen some real bean eaters in my time but nothing to equal this. These dudes were champions.

There is always a reason to every thing a cowboy does. Even to little things. A cow hand sits on his hocks when he eats as a chair is unknown in camp. I thought, of courst, the reason the dudes all stood up to feed was because of the shortage of chairs. It wasn't until I dug up a saddle blanket for my dude to sit on that I found I was mistaken.

My fat dude was a friendly dude an' a mighty polite dude too. But the blanket, he said, was out. An' he added too that even if there was a rocker in camp he was too tender behind to use it.

After supper all of the dudes stood around the fire an' talked while the punchers sat on their hocks. It was a right smart gathering too. We found dudes in camp from most every where when we went to checking up.

New York, Boston, Chicago, Pittsburgh, Pa., St. Louis and Baltimore were all represented there. There was one dude from Philadelphia, Pa., who went to sleep standing up. The puncher who was herding him couldn't figger his dude out. He said this dude had been dead on his feet from the time he left the ranch.

There were two dudes from Wilmington, Delaware. I

thought they were spoofing at first. I had never heard of the place. It wasn't until they dug up a road map an' proved it that we knew there was such a state. But it was nothing to brag about as far as any of us cow hands could see. We could have dumped the state of Delaware in the calf pasture at the Bar X Ranch an' never have seen it again.

There were a couple of dudes from Moline, Illinois, an' sporty dudes they were. Some of the cow hands thought they were spoofing too but I had heard of that town. I onct knew a Mormon Nester near Gila Bend who had bought a plow from that place.

There was only one dude in the lay-out who really burnt us out. He was a Los Angeles dude. The night he drove into the ranch he began talking about the climate there before he got out of his car. An' onct in the ranch house no matter what the talk this dude would horn right in. Balky said he heard him talking about the California climate in his sleep after the dude had bedded. Naturally, none of the cow hands wanted to herd this dude an' get hisself talked to death. We finally cut cards for him. I came mighty close to getting him as I cut the trey of hearts an' don't think it wasn't a relief to me when Shorty Caraway cut a duce.

Shorty said they had no more than left the ranch than this dude opened up. He turned both barrels loose at onct an' what's more he kept it up. According to this dude any one who didn't live in Southern California was only half alive. It was really the promised land. It was the state where Moses was heading for when he led his children forth. There was no snow or frost or desert winds. Although it misted some it wouldn't wet a man as it never really rained an' the sun shone all the time. Any man you met would be your friend an' money grew on trees.

But Shorty had been to California onct hisself with a load

of Cross S steers. He finally told this dude about his trip an' Shorty told the dude if there was any money growing it hadn't sprouted yet when he was over there an' what's more it had rained when he was over there an' it wasn't a dry rain either as he got wet as hell. But Shorty did meet a friend. In fact he met two of them an' these two slicks picked Shorty clean before he came back home.

But it didn't even faze the dude. He had no sense of shame. That night as the dudes all stood around the fire an' talked the California dude would horn right in no matter what the subject was an' talk about his climate.

That night before they bedded the dudes got down their bets. When I found they were laying bets on No. 2 I got one down myself with Balky Bill who was herding the Chicago dude. Balky thought he was pretty hot but from what I had seen on No. 1 I was stringing with my dude. I finally bet Balky a dollar a hole an' ten more that we would beat them in. When the Chicago dude heard about it he wanted to bet hisself.

This Chicago dude was a sporty dude but he had nothing on mine. He didn't any more than get his roll out until my dude snapped it up. They agreed to play for ten dollars a hole an' they put up an extra hundred that was to go to the first dude who tapped his ball into the can at the 18th hole at the ranch.

I kept thinking Cat Claw would come in even after we had bedded the dudes. I waited up a while, there was still some coffee in the pot and I kept playing it. I thought I heard Cat Claw's pony coming at least a dozen times but it was really hard to cock an ear on account of the sleeping dudes.

Most of them slept like drunks but several tossed about an' muttered in their sleep. There was one dude who thought he was out on the courst still battling with his niblick.

We started the second hole next morning just as soon as it broke light. The wrangler brought the horses in with the rising of the morning star. While the punchers saddled horses Cookie routed out the dudes. Some were so goggle-eyed with sleep they didn't know where they were an' the cook had to throw a pail of water over two of them before they could be woke.

The dudes were supposed to start in the order they had finished but things were all balled up. When the dude who had finished fourth could not be found we didn't know what to think. The puncher who was herding him was sure that he had bedded his dude the night before. We finally found this dude wandering about in a cholla thicket just outside of camp talking to hisself. Another dude went back to bed an' dared the cook to rouse him. But this dude didn't know a round-up cook and he soon came out of it.

I've handled cattle all my life in every kind of weather but moving these dudes off the bed ground was the worst job I ever had. They moved fourteen different ways at onct. Just when we thought we had our dudes strung out a couple would lay down. One dude I caught who was heading back towards the ranch house was walking in his sleep.

It was no use to try to herd the dudes afoot so all of the punchers mounted. An' I doubt if we would ever have got our dudes off the bed ground if it wasn't for Wicker Bill's pony. Wicker always rides a snake. As soon as Wicker topped him off the pony came unwound. The pony bucked right into camp bellering like a steer.

He scattered the pots an' pans four ways at onct an' upset the coffee pot. The cook was fit to be tied. But at least it got the dudes awake enough that we could get them started.

I finally herded my fat dude to the tee. He was the first to shoot. And it looked to me as if I had made a bad bet with Balky Bill that morning when we started.

It wasn't that my dude dubbed his tee shot that worried me. That was to be expected as my dude seemed in a daze. An' one bad shot more or less doesn't make much difference with fifteen miles to play. But my dude was so stiff an' sore from his ride the day previous that he couldn't mount his horse.

With fifteen long hard miles ahead of us I was feeling pretty sick. It looked as if my dude had petered out before he was even started. But after the sun got up a ways he seemed more like hisself. When I looked back an' saw the other dudes strung out I felt a whole lot better. Every man jack among the dudes was walking and leading his horse.

The play on No. 1 had been a lead pipe cinch to what lay ahead of them. While No. 1 was a longer hole by several miles there wasn't really any hazards. No. 2 was really rough and up hill all the way. My fat dude had lost twenty balls the first half mile he played.

At the rate my dude was losing balls I knew he would never finish as he only had a peck. When we talked the situation over he admitted it looked serious to him. It was then I put it up to him about using better balls. And my dude was really skeptical about this dog of mine.

But it was a groundhog case as far as my dude went. There was nothing else to do. He finally took my say so. After I loped back an' got a dozen Kroflites offn the cook Top Flite went to work.

I packed my fat dude's canteen for him so's he wouldn't run out of water. I watched him pretty close as the sun got overhead. At intervals I'd water him an' make him stop an' get his breath whether he wanted to or not. But he was pulling on the bitts from the time he started out. It was hard to get him held up long enough to even take a breather.

When he rested it was with one eye cocked upon the hill

below. At the first sound of a dude behind us he would grab a club an' start. I hadn't watched him very long until I knew that Dad was right when he said that the tougher the courst an' the more misery a dude could deal hisself the better he liked the game.

My dude admitted that my hunch about the golf balls was working out all right. No matter where he socked a ball my dog would find it for him. Buck brush, cat claw thickets, cholla, ocatillos an' prickly pear an' thickets of just plain cactus were all about us now. My dude never missed a thicket as he worked his way along.

Just to watch my golf houn' work that day would have gladdened any golfer's heart. My dude said if I would only sell the dog he would take him East with him. It was plenty tough on Top Flite too the punishment he took. As we worked our way on up the ridge I watered Top Flite now each time I did my dude.

The place where Black Canyon cuts in on No. 2 is what I'd really call a hazard. Of courst, any dude could play the ridge but even then he couldn't play it safe as the ridge is very narrow. By shooting acrost the canyon he could save at least two miles.

The canyon in the shortest place is just a hundred yards. But if a man don't reach the other side he's just a blowed up sucker. The bottom of the canyon is five hundred feet below. It's just another lost ball for a dude unless he has a dog.

Before he tried the shot I watered my dude out again an' made him rest a while. But he was in such a hurry to take a shot at it he wouldn't take his time.

My dude was so excited now he shook from head to foot. He finally turned away. I told him not to look below if it upset his stomach. He said of all the places he had been he had never seen its like. I wanted to tell him then he hadn't seen nothing yet. But he was shaking as it was so I thought I'd better not.

When he finally gathered hisself together an' teed up I was hoping for the best but he topped the doggone thing. It must have landed on a rock as we could hear the "crack" below a good half minute later. Then my dude teed up another one an' topped his ball again.

He was getting hot and bothered now an' shooting too darn fast. He wouldn't keep his head down long enough to see what he was doing. I finally talked him into setting down an' cooling off a bit as he had one Kroflite left. This time he kept the old bean down an' put this one acrost.

We lost a good half hour while Top Flite hunted balls. An' my dog's tongue was hanging out at least a foot when he brought up the last one. The Chicago dude an' Balky came in sight just as we moved on. Since they didn't have a golf houn' I wasn't worried any.

The bet I had that day with Balky Bill looked pretty good right then. My dude had the jack pot as good as won if I could only keep him moving.

The last few miles were pretty rough but we finally made it in. Top Flite never lost a ball although some were badly battered an' considerable out of shape. My dude was just about all in but he finished on his feet. Considering the fact that he had hoofed it all the way I gave that hombre credit.

My dude was fed and bedded down before the Chicago dude got in. And this Chicago dude didn't stand around the fire an' talk when he had finished eating. Our dudes were both asleep an' sawing wood when Shorty an' his Los Angeles dude came over the brow of the hill.

An' this Los Angeles dude really finished strong. I'll give him credit for that. An' that hombre never even opened up his trap while Shorty was feeding him. Shorty bedded his dude

without a word from him. It was really hard to believe. But this Los Angeles dude was sleeping like a drunken man as soon as Shorty got him covered.

It was late that night before the other dudes came in but all of them finished that night. It was near midnight when Wicker Bill came in with my fat dude's New York pardner. He was the last dude in an' he was the only dude to finish mounted.

Wicker had him crossways on his horse an' Wicker had throwed a diamond hitch about him to keep him from falling off. He was completely out.

(6)

THAT NIGHT IN CAMP at Alkali was the worst night I ever put in. To hear the dudes calling for water through the night was pitiful to me. I had nursed my fat dude's canteen along the day before but it was pretty low. It was only when my dude could stand it no longer that I gave him a little water. Then I only let him have a few drops at a time — just enough to wet his tongue an' throat. I wanted to save enough for at least one good drink for myself before we started out next morning.

It was really tough on some of the dudes who had no water left. They had all been warned, of courst. Yet some of them had drunk a full canteen while playing No. 2. The cook at Alkali had a barrel of water but he wouldn't put any out. It was all the water he an' the wrangler would have to drink themselves until they packed in another barrel.

I thought the break of day would never come. Between getting up and down to wet my fat dude's tongue an' the cries of the dudes about me I didn't get much sleep. Balky Bill who did a hitch of eighteen months in France said he never put in a night while he was over there that had anything on this.

Moving our dudes off the bed ground that morning was even worse than the previous day an' breakfast was out of the question. With the cook standing guard over his water barrel with a 30-30 we could get no water to throw. Even when we mounted our dudes refused to string out. To complicate matters still further Wicker's pony refused to buck. We worked for a good half hour but trying to move our dudes in a herd wouldn't work at all.

In handling wild cattle when they bush up there is only one thing to do. It is only used as a last resort as it's pretty rough on the stock. But there was no other out that we could see an' the punchers were all agreed that the only thing left was to rope our dudes an' lead them to the tee.

My fat dude was the first to start again as he had finished first an' my fat dude didn't fight the rope. He seemed only in a daze. It wasn't until I teed a ball up for him an' put his driver in his hands that my fat dude seemed to realize what was expected of him.

Without as much as a practise swing he wound up in a knot an' let go. An' there was a crack like the report of a forty-five when the club head came into the ball. It was the doggondest lick my dude had made in the two days he had played. An' the doggondest lick I had ever seen since our outfit took up golf.

Day was just breaking through the hills an' the light was so poor I couldn't follow the entire flight of the ball. But it started low an' straight like the flight of a quail, gradually rising all the time. There wasn't even a semblance of a slice. He had finally hit one straight — when it faded out of sight the little pill was still rising.

It was the kind of a shot that would make any golfer shout for joy. I yelled long and loud myself an' the punchers who had seen an' heard this lick cut loose like a bunch of coyotes. We had never seen Jones or Hagen or Andra Kirkaldy play. But we knew that none of those curly wolves had ever struck a better blow in their lives.

The outfit was all about him now slapping my dude on the back. An' my dude didn't seem to realize what he had done as he stood in a sort of daze.

I finally took his driver from his hand an' placed it in his bag. When we started my dude began to walk an' lead his horse like he had the previous day. But on the strength of the blow my dude had struck I hoisted him into the saddle.

When they saw my fat dude mounted once more the outfit gave him a cheer. But it never even fazed my dude. His expression never changed.

He sat his horse like a wooden Indian. If I hadn't known my dude so well I would have sworn this lick he had made was a common thing with him. This was before I realized my dude was really unconscious an' playing as if in his sleep.

No. 3 is down hill all of the way. Even a topped shot will roll for a mile an' knowing the blow my dude had struck I put my pony into a trot. At which my fat dude's pony trotted too. But even this jolting my dude got didn't bring him out of his daze.

I would hate to say offhand just how far my dude's drive went. An' since I've learned that all golfers are always prone to overestimate the length of a shot an' exaggerate I wont attempt it here. But it is enough to say that the pokes on No. 3 have been plenty long since we put in the courst. An' there has never been a blow struck yet that could equal the drive of my dude's.

With both our ponies trotting we were making good time. But I finally pulled my pony down to a walk when I saw that my fat dude was trying to shake hisself to death. For a little spell I was afraid I had overestimated this drive my dude had made. I was afraid we had over rode the ball until I heard Top Flite barking treed, at least a good half mile below.

The ball had lodged in a pile of rock that finally stopped its roll. When we rode up Top Flite wagged his tail as proud as he could be. It wasn't until I teed the ball up for my dude that my dog quit barking treed—at least, that's what this particular bark is called when a dog has located a varmit. Not knowing any better word to use I use the term myself. Although I realize to some it may sound a little strange.

When I remarked to my dude that if it wasn't for this

particular pile of rock where the ball had lodged it would have been good for another quarter at least, he showed no interest whatever. It wasn't until I had pulled him off his horse an' put his brassie in his hand that he come out of it again.

Owing to the fact our courst was new Dad had ordered winter rules. Several of the dudes told him it was a common thing back East on courses that were new. Although it wasn't so sporty Dad favored this rule hisself. From what he had seen Dad knew that not even cactus would ever grow again where a dude had used his niblick.

When I teed up my fat dude's ball for him he came alive again. There was another crack like a pistol shot. My dude had done it again! He had struck two potent blows without the sign of a practise swing. An' what's more he had struck these mighty blows without the sign of a slice.

As my dude was only playing against time I didn't count his strokes that day. I've always been sorry too as it would have stood for some kind of a record on the courst. Not onct did my dude miss the ball completely on his swing. Not onct did he pop one up or top a ball an' never onct did he slice. That in itself is some kind of a record too. But the unusual thing about it to me was the fact that my dude was doing it unconsciously. He was really playing unconscious golf as he was practically out on his feet.

We could have made a record too in time that day if my dude could have trotted his horse. I tried it several times but each time on looking at my dude I pulled my pony down to a walk. It wasn't done purposely on his part, of that much I was sure. An' still it looked to me as if my dude was deliberately trying to shake hisself to death each time his pony trotted.

My dude had used nothing but a wood since we left the

tee. They were quail shots every one. Starting low an' rising slowly until they faded out of view. It wasn't until we sighted the green not over a quarter of a mile below us that I handed my dude a mashie when I unloaded him to shoot.

The mashie was really my mistake. I should have slipped my dude his niblick as he overshot the green. Since it was uphill coming back he had some little trouble.

But my dude had been fed an' watered. I let him drink his fill. An' he was asleep just as soon as I bedded him with the sun still overhead.

The cook an' the horse wrangler on No. 3 were both new men with the outfit. I knew them both as punchers, of courst, but neither the cook or the wrangler had ever played golf in their life. I was practising on No. 3 green with my fat dude's putter trying to improve my putting a little an' showing them how it was done. When these two birds got interested an' wanted to play it looked pretty soft to me.

Just to make it light on the boys we shot for ten cents a hole. An' was that third green fast? There was really no way of holeing a putt unless you stroked the ball. It was the thing that Scotty MacDonald preached to Balky an' me when he gave us our lessons on Stray Horse. "The stroke is the thing," says Scotty, an' he certainly proved it to us.

But as long as I'd paid for my lessons I could see no reason why the cook an' the wrangler shouldn't put out a bit for theirs. But the best I could say for both of these birds was that they were terrible.

The cook putted clear off the green the first four times he tried it. Although the wrangler did accidentally hole one on his second shot when he raised his head an' topped it.

I had just got into the wrangler for a dollar six bits an' the cook owed me an even two bucks. Both of these birds were so bad I began to feel sorry for them. In fact, they were so helpless I was just showing the cook how to take his stance an' take the putter back real slow an' to let the blade follow through the ball when something went whizzing overhead like the buzz of an angry bee.

At sound of it the wrangler took to the brush an' the cook went flat on the ground. Then realizing he was still exposed he tried to crawl into the cup. Neither of these waddies had been overseas but they had worked in Old Mexico.

Every Arizona puncher who has ever branded a neighbor's calf knows the whine of a 30-30 slug an' the buzz of a forty-five. An' it's a sound he doesn't enjoy. But as long as I couldn't get into the cup with the cook I had to hunt for my cover elsewhere. I was making my sneak as best I could, crawling along like a snake. I had almost reached the big Sycamore at the edge of the green when another one went over.

When I heard a crack below us like a pistol shot I thought whoever it was was trying to take the camp was shooting from that way too. I had just decided to take a chance an' make a run for my horse when a golf ball rolled onto the green. It was a whippet too.

The wrangler who had took to the brush had got plumb out of hearing. When I told Cookie it was just some of the dudes on the hill above making their approach shots he wouldn't believe me at first. I was helping him out of his hole when another one whizzed overhead an' too blame close for comfort.

The cook dove for the cup again but he realized by now it didn't afford much cover. An' he wanted to make a run for it hoping to reach the brush. Even after he learned what the shooting was it had the hombre spooked.

He claimed that a golf ball would kill a man just as quick as a bullet. A golf ball was bigger too an' as far as he could tell there wasn't the slightest difference in the sound when one went whizzing over.

There was something to this talk of his an' I agreed with him but since he had never seen golf played I figgered a little different. I knew the dudes were shooting for the green. From what I'd seen of golf this far I knew the cook an' I were safer where we were as we were in the center.

But even against my say so Cookie wanted to run. It was all I could do to hold him down until the thing was over. An' my judgment proved correct. The cook admitted it hisself as the next two shots went over high an' way off to the right.

The punchers all thought it right funny when we told them what had occurred. It wasn't until a ball whizzed over as we talked that they accepted our point of view.

We finally posted a man on the brow of the hill. He was to flag every outfit down before their approach was made. An' he was to tell every puncher not to slip his dude anything except a niblick on this shot. As we knew if the dudes kept using woods from there it would only be a question of time before they finally killed some one.

If every golf hole was down hill there would be nothing to the game. The sun was still four hours high when the last dude in that day had been watered, fed an' bedded.

Although none of the dudes stood about the fire an' talked on looking them over as they fed they appeared in better shape than they were the previous night. In spite of the fact that some of them especially my fat dude had shed considerable weight.

All of them had finished fairly strong at least they were on their feet. Even my fat dude's pardner who had been carried in the night before was moving about although he still limped a bit.

It was only the fact that the Los Angeles dude wasn't

talking yet that made us realize that our dudes weren't really normal. An' we should watch them pretty clost. We knew as soon as that hombre started to talk again everything would be jake.

(7)

WHEN THE WRANGLER didn't come in after the shooting it was up to one of us to look after the saddle horses. When we cut the cards I lost. By the time I had hobbled the ponies and got back to camp the outfit had started a putting game. It was going strong.

The game had started at five cents a shot. Then they raised the ante to ten. By the time I had got back an' into the game it had jumped to two bits a putt. As I knew the green pretty well from my previous session with the horse wrangler an' cook I didn't do so bad. As a matter of fact I had it all my way while the game was two bits a throw.

There were fourteen cow hands besides the cook an' he was really fish. Occasionally a hand would get froze out as this game was strictly cash. When someone suggested we kick it up to four bits a putt it suited me exactly. But when we raised the ante Balky Bill got hot.

I never saw the like of the way they rolled for that lucky stiff. Where a putt of mine would curl away from the cup one of his would curl right in. We tried it from every place on the green. Balky's luck still held. When some waddie suggested we raise the ante to six bits I welcomed it myself. Anything to change the run of the luck would have been all right with me.

As I figgered the luck did change but it didn't come to me. It went to Shorty Caraway. He was worse than Balky Bill. There were only ten cow hands left in the game, the rest were all froze out. But with ten men each kicking in six bits a putt it made a very soothing pot.

At least half of the pots that Shorty won were really nothing but luck. He never stroked a putt. All Shorty did was to shut his eyes an' bang away an' into the cup the ball would go for another seven-fifty.

It finally got so dark we had decided to quit. The game had really broke up when someone suggested we try just one more an' make it a dollar this time.

We putted from twenty feet. The light was pretty poor. It was all any one could do to see the cup but the putts were very clost. There wasn't a ball in the outfit over two feet from the cup. I thought I had it in the bag when my putt rimmed the can. But as it hung just on the lip it still looked good to me. To beat it a putt would have to drop. There was just one more man to shoot. He was the cook on No. 3 an' he was terrible.

He hadn't sunk a putt since the game began a good four hours before. Every one else no matter how lousy he was had won at least two pots. That hombre had me really feeling sorry for him. He was really fish. I had already counted up the ten as won an' I hadn't done so bad. But the thing that makes golf the game it is was the fact that there is nothing certain about it.

The cook didn't even know what we meant by a stance. If he had he couldn't have took it. He putted much like Shorty did, he was really unconscious about it. All there was to it as far as he knew was to shut his eyes an' shoot.

An' that is just what Cookie did. He just up an' banged away. If his ball hadn't hit the back of the cup it would have rolled clear off the green. An' Cookie really hit the back of the cup, there was no doubt about it. The ball bounced at least two feet in the air then fell back in for a win.

We started late next morning. The sun was almost up. We supposed, of courst, the wrangler would come back in the night but that hombre never came in. Having seen him as he started he was heading south right then. I figgered if he held his courst he should have crossed the line into Mexico long before we were up.

But some one had to bring in the horses. Since I hobbled them out the night before every one looked to me an' as usual when I wrangle they were scattered from hell to breakfast an' caused me considerable grief.

The dudes had all been fed when I got into camp. Some of them went back to the bed ground while we were saddling up. But as we had quit trying to move them in a herd we

didn't have much trouble. Each puncher simply caught his dude an' led him to the tee.

My dude was the first to shoot again. When I teed his ball up for him an' put his driver in his hands he struck another potent lick. He started to walk an' lead his horse as he left the tee so I boosted him into the saddle. But he got no cheer from the outfit as he had the previous day. The blows my dude was striking was becoming common with him.

It was almost too much for me to expect that he would do it two days in a row. But that was just what he did. Every blow he struck was right on the nose without the sign of a slice. They were quail shots every one. No. 4, the Rock Creek hole, is plenty tough because of the winding creek. But I doubt if my dude even saw the creek that day the way that he was playing.

A brassie, an iron or a niblick were all the same to him. No matter which club I slipped him he banged the old ball on the nose. I had got a dozen new Kroflites offn the cook for him as the old balls were pretty well battered an' considerable out of shape. Top Flite never lost a ball that day. I was certainly proud of him.

We were held up almost an hour on No. 4 but it wasn't my fat dude's fault. It was just above the steer trap about two miles above the green that we met the old black bear. Top Flite had just located a ball an' was barking treed although we couldn't see the dog. It wasn't until we come over the brow of the hill that I saw the old bear and her cubs.

The old black sister had two cubs an' she was really on the prod. Top Flite's barking when he found the ball might have stirred her up. Nine times out of ten a bear will run whenever they wind a man. Fact is, a man must lean forward on his horse when he is following one.

It might have been the fact that she had cubs then again it might have been my dude. While she had seen cow-punchers from time to time a dude was something strange. At any rate the old black sister didn't want to move an' she certainly took her own sweet time in getting out of our way.

I was packing a 30-30 so there was nothing to worry about. But as long as she had two cubs I didn't want to take a shot if it wasn't necessary. There was nothing to do but set down an' wait until she moseyed on her way. That was just what we done. Our ponies, of courst, both snorted an' plunged. But my fat dude sat there just as unconcerned as if he didn't see her.

The sun was less than an hour high when we got in that night. It was dark when the last dude got in. I had hoped that the outfit would get in in time for another game of freeze-out. I managed to get a little practise though an' try out No. 4 green. After I fed an' bedded my dude I borrowed his putter again.

With dudes coming in every little while the wrangler had to put out their horses. He didn't get to try it. But after watching me tap a few balls into the can the cook got interested. Since he had never tried it before we only putted for ten cents a throw so's to make it light on him. We didn't get to play very long, not over an hour I guess. But as long as I won two bucks from the cook I suppose I shouldn't complain.

Handling our dudes the way we did there was nothing to it now. As No. 5 was a breather we got in early that night. We had four hours of good daylight after the last dude was in an' the freeze-out game at No. 5 was something to talk about.

We started as usual at five cents. The game soon jumped to ten. By the time we had putted around five times it jumped to a half a dollar. An' was I warm on No. 5? I hope to tell a man. I had froze the whole blame outfit out before the game could jump to a dollar.

It was one of those days that every golfer hopes for an' which seldom if ever come. Somehow I couldn't have missed a putt that day if I had really tried. Everything Scotty had showed me worked out as smooth as silk. The line of each putt was as plain to me as a cow trail through the sand.

I took the club head back with my left hand, slow. Then let it follow through, the pendulum on Grandma's clock had nothing on me that day. At last I had found the secret. I had the old game licked an' I told the outfit so. But they said it was all boloney an' really nothing but luck.

It was dawn on the morning of the sixth day out. We were starting No. 6 hole. Every thing was in order an' going smooth when Shorty's Los Angeles dude looked around wild-eyed an' wanted to know where he was. Shorty was quiet an' easy with him an' explained in a quiet voice that he was playing golf at the Bar X Ranch an' was just ready to start the 6th hole. It was the first word his dude had spoken since that day on No. 2.

We knew he was coming out of it. It wouldn't be long now. My dude hadn't spoken yet but when he sliced his drive that morning we knew it was only a question of a little time until all of our dudes would be back to normal again an' completely out of their daze.

The No. 6 hole isn't much at best an' while there is plenty of water such as it is it doesn't make much of a camp. An' to make matters worse the night we got into Stinking Springs on the sixth supper wasn't ready an' the cook could not be found.

When I couldn't find the wrangler I didn't know what to think. I got in first with my dude an' rustled up some chuck.

When Balky got in with his Chicago dude he looked after the saddle horses.

There was something queer about the whole thing we couldn't figger out. Both of their saddles were in camp an' while Balky was putting our horses out he found their hobbled horses. It was hard to believe they had pulled out afoot with two horses in sight of camp. We hollered an' Balky shot his six shooter off a dozen times but we couldn't raise any one.

Next morning I cooked breakfast while Balky was hunting horses. We had just saddled up an' were moving our dudes off the bed ground to the tee when the cook staggered into camp.

At sight of the cook there wasn't a dude in the layout who didn't come alive right now. The Chicago dude who was supposed to be tough would have took to the brush if he could. The dudes had seen some of the Apache Indians about the ranch an' it was only natural that they should think the Apaches had took to the war path. After I took another look at the cook I didn't blame the dudes. It wasn't until the cook got clost enough that I could get a whiff of him that I guessed what the trouble was. It was perfectly simple then.

To make a short story out of a long one, the cook had been drunk an' fighting with the horse wrangler who was still asleep in the brush. The two of them had been alone in camp five days so a fight was to be expected.

But the thing that none of the punchers could figger out was where the liquor come from. We knew these two right well. An' it would have been impossible for them to have packed enough liquor in on a horse to keep both of them drunk five days.

I think it was the scare on No. 6 as much as anything that brought our dudes around. Shorty said his Los Angeles dude began talking that morning an' kept it up all day. At any rate he was going strong that night on No. 7. He said of all the place he had ever been, Arizona had the lousiest climate. "Now the climate in California," he says, but that was when I walked out. It was dark when we finished the hole but the moon was full that night an' just as soon as the moon came up we started a little freeze-out. Or rather it was just a putting game at ten cents an' since I had all the money it had to be on credit.

An' my fat dude was really hisself that day. He began with another slice an' what's more he didn't hit a straight one all day long. He was back to his same old round-house.

It was the first time he had spoken to me since that day on No. 2 an' as he played along on No. 7 that day we had a regular visit.

He admitted that he thought cowpunchers were a strange breed before he came to the ranch. The fact that he was curious about us was one of the reasons he came. From little remarks that he let slip his ideas had been queer. He seemed surprised that the outfit had been together just a week without some one getting shot. I guess he was surprised that none of us were haired-over an' lived by eating grass. It was when he got strung out on golf that I liked my fat dude best.

My fat dude had read Morrison too an' we augered quite a bit. I held out for the overlapping grip Jones used while my fat dude interlocked. My dude held with the cook back at the Headquarters ranch that the proper pointing of the chin was the secret of all good golf. Like Cookie, he would point his chin as well as any man until he started to make his swing. That was when the rub began, he couldn't keep it pointed.

I don't guess there had ever been a prize golfer who my fat dude hadn't seen. He spoke of one Eyetalian named Sarazen who was a curly wolf at the game. It was the first I realized that the game had spread so much. But it was something for my dude to have seen the champion of Italy.

According to my dude he had played most everywhere. Of all the courses he had played back East he liked Pine Valley best. He said Pine Valley was really nothing as compared to our courst here. He had never seen as sporty a hole as the first one out from the ranch. That surprised me in a way as it was nothing to No. 2. An' come to find out he didn't remember it at all.

When I told him he had won six jack pots in a row an' that he was six up on the Chicago dude he wouldn't believe me at first. It wasn't until the punchers verified it that he would believe the yarn.

When I told him about the blow he had struck that morning on No. 3 he thought I was spoofing him. The fact that he had went three days without the sign of a slice was too much for him to believe. Even when the punchers vouched for it my fat dude shook his head. Stretching the truth in some cases was all right, he said, but there was a limit to everything.

What really surprised my dude was the fact we enjoyed the game. My dude had some sweet clubs too. Each club was numbered an' marked with the range as to just how far it would shoot.

None of our clubs from Buck an' Sears were marked in this way at all. It was when I mentioned this to my dude that he said if he could only beat this Chicago dude in that he would buy me a set of Tom Boy Irons an' a set of Hagen Woods.

Even when the Chicago dude beat us in that night I wasn't worried none. We were still five up on him. An' those new clubs my dude had promised me were as good as in the bag.

(8)

WE FINISHED THE FIRST NINE HOLES in just nine days. My dude was still three up an' my fat dude was a different man when we started the second nine. I didn't have to lead him to the tee no more with both of his eyes swelled shut. Instead of pouring water over him in the morning to get him awake he rolled out of his own accord. He was always right on tap to eat as soon as the cook yelled chuck.

He had lost the fat an' pasty look he had when he first started. He was brown as an Apache Indian. His eye was clear an' bright although they still watered some on cold mornings an' on days when the wind blew hard. But a sand-storm will make even a cowboy bleary-eyed. That was to be expected. He was getting used to riding too. His blisters were all gone. He had almost come to the place where he could swing off an' onto his horse again like a Rodeo relay rider. The only thing that worried me was the way he was shedding weight.

He began to really take an interest in the things about him now. Instead of falling asleep as he ate I didn't have to bed him no more. He had reached the place where he would sometimes set up an' talk for a spell after his evening meal. He was conscious of things about him now he hadn't seen before. When he told me one day that this Los Angeles dude an' his talk was the only thing that got on his nerves I knew he was back to normal.

It was as if he had never seen the first gray streaks of dawn or the break of day in the hills. A coyote slipping along thru the half light or a band of wild horses a mile away was enough to start him off.

The day we sighted the bear on No. 9 he almost went hogwild. To have seen a bear on a golf courst would be something to tell back East. It was only a half grown bear at that an' we didn't see much of him. This fellow had winded us an' was on his way before we sighted him. When I told my dude we had been held up for an hour on No. 4 by an old bear an' two cubs he thought I was spoofing again. No sir, he hadn't even seen the old black sister an' her two cubs that held us up that day.

When I spoke of our trouble in crossing Black Canyon on No. 2 he looked at me sort of blank. Yet he remembered the first hole he had played even to little details. He remembered Cat Claw coming back an' wanting to borrow some golf balls when his long hitting dude ran out. He even asked what had become of them. As I hadn't see hide nor hair of either one I didn't know myself.

My dude could remember the first hole. Everything else was blank until we left Stinking Springs that morning to start the 7th hole. The first thing that had registered was when the cook came out of the brush.

Now that he was out of his daze my dude was good company too. But in one way it would have suited me more to have had him unconscious again. The tenth hole was perfectly simple if a man could hit a straight ball. I hate to think how many balls we lost that day on No. 10.

It was no use to use a good ball as even Top Flite couldn't work. Once a ball went over the rim of Devil's Canyon even a golf houn' couldn't find it. It was just as bad on No. 11 which follows the canyon back. My dude had more than a slice on those two holes, it was really a regular old round-house.

The way Balky's Chicago dude was creeping up had me worried too. My dude hadn't won a hole from him since the one at Stinking Springs. It looked to me as if I was ready to kiss my new clubs adios before I got holt of them.

At least there was one thing to be thankful for. Balky's Chicago dude an' mine had both gained a hole on the other dudes. When we played No. 9 our dudes were the only two

to finish the hole that day. An' I didn't have to listen to the Los Angeles dude any more at night around the fire.

At first I missed the freeze-out game each night when we got in. But since the game was on credit now it was just as well, I guess. An' with only two dudes to look after in camp the cook an' the horse wrangler had plenty of time when we got in at night. There was only one draw back to the thing. Since Balky an' his Chicago dude were getting into camp ahead of us Balky often had those birds picked clean before I got into the game.

But the way my dude was shedding weight was becoming

serious. His clothes were becoming a problem too. They were just a hanging on him. It was only after I cut off my saddle strings an' rigged up some suspenders for him that I knew he wouldn't lose his rompers.

But in spite of the weight my dude had shed he said he was feeling fine an' he really believed he was in better shape than he had been in twenty years. He said too that he would be willing to lose this hundred he bet with the Chicago dude if he could shed off ten more pounds. But when I reminded him I had a bet on him myself with Balky Bill he said he wouldn't throw me down.

Any one to play the last nine coming in had to be in shape. The first nine was only a breather compared to the second nine. The first hole my dude won on the second nine was the day we played the twelfth. It was that day in camp at No. 12 that I got this hunch of mine.

The talk in camp that night at No. 12 was about the 13th hole that we would play next day. I tried to head it off as best I could but I didn't get anywhere.

The cook said the river was higher than he had seen it in four years. It would be swimming water for at least a hundred yards. He spoke of how much the heavy rains back up in the mountains had done for the C Dart Range. It had put out several forest fires. Yes, the rain had been a Godsend.

Since this talk wasn't enough to scare a dude to death to help it along the wrangler spoke of ten head of C Dart steers he had seen the previous day. They had floated past him in twenty minutes time an' all ten head were drowned. When I pooh-poohed such talk the wrangler got on the peck. That dumbbell didn't even get my sign when I tried to shut him up.

I winked at my fat dude too as if the talk was all a joke, as if it were done to tamp him. An' thank God my dude had heard punchers talk so much since he had started out he really believed they were lieing. He laughed an' passed it off hisself as if it was all a joke. But just the same by little things he said an' certain little moves he made I knew this talk all had him plenty spooked an' he was really nervous.

This Chicago dude wasn't really bothered none. At least from the way he talked. This dude said he wasn't afraid of water no how as he could swim just like a duck. He said Chicago was by a lake so big you couldn't see acrost. He didn't say that he had swum acrost this lake but he did say that when he was home he swam there every day.

He really didn't seem to be afraid of water none. I watched him as he talked. It wasn't until he pulled the one about the lake so big you couldn't see the other side I figgered he was lieing.

It was while this talk was going round that I figgered out my plan. If I could only get my dude to the water's edge before it was light enough for him to see what he was up against I knew I'd be all right. Of courst, the old mine cable could be used as a last resort. It was really safe. But by shooting him acrost on it we would lose at least an hour. We were still one up an' I didn't intend for my dude to lose if there was any way about it. I didn't enjoy the idea of swimming the river none too much myself. But with a chance to win a new set of clubs as well as the bet I had with Balky Bill I would have taken a chance on swimming this lake the Chicago dude spoke about.

I routed my fat dude out next morning long before the morning star appeared. I had been up an hour already. As it's considerable trouble hunting horses in the dark an' I didn't want to wake the wrangler. That goof would have spilled the beans. The first thing that dead-head would have wanted to know was why we were starting so early.

I put on the coffee pot when I left the camp. It had boiled when I got back an' I woke my dude as easy as possible so's not to rouse the camp. The wrangler an' cook both slept like drunks. Balky, of courst, knew some one was up but he didn't dream it was me. He thought it was only the cook stirring around throwing the breakfast together. Not knowing what it was all about my fat dude, of courst, was curious. It wasn't until I shisshed him several times that he quit trying to ask me questions.

My dude couldn't eat the cold steak an' biscuits an' cold beans were out for him. He didn't really want any coffee.

But I kept after him until he downed at least a quart of it. I knew he would need it later.

I had saddled our horses out of camp. When my fat dude could get no more coffee down I motioned him to follow. An' that hombre made enough noise getting out of camp to wake a dozen outfits. The first thing he did was to bang his foot against a dutch oven an' knock off the lid. Then he knocked over a pot of beans. Judging from the noise he made he didn't miss stepping on one dry leaf or twig in the hundred yards we traveled an' in spite of all the noise he made our luck held up that morning. The cook an' the wrangler slept like drunks. Balky thought it was only the cook in a little worse humor than usual.

Once we were mounted my fat dude wanted to know what it was all about. He spoke in whispers, of courst. But it wasn't until we were out of hearing of the camp that I told him what the big idea was an' then I lied to him.

I told him we were just copping a sneak on Balky an' his Chicago dude. There was no rule I had ever heard of to keep a man from starting before day break if he felt like starting early.

As he had no doubt gathered from the talk, the 13th hole was tough. All the talk about the river was bunk, of courst, but the hole itself was hard. With an early start we should win the 13th easy, granted our luck held up. To be two up with only four to play was a very soothing lead.

There was another thing besides the river on my mind but I didn't mention it either. I knew the cook an' the horse wrangler on the 13th hole were both new men who had never played any golf. If we got in early enough I knew I could pick both of these birds before Balky got into the game.

Climbing Squaw Peak in the dark afoot was all of an hour's hard work. There were several places where I gave my fat dude a hand as any kind of a little slip meant a drop of a thousand feet. The more I saw of the climb the smarter I knew my hunch had been in starting my dude early. It was just as well it was dark. Since Black Canyon on No. 2 upset his stomach, I knew my dude would have layed right down an' died if he could have seen the drop below him.

We took a breather on reaching the top. Both of us needed it. The morning star had not appeared. Our luck was holding out. I teed the ball up for my dude an' he got ready with his spoon. It was the only club I let him pack as we climbed up the butte. It was a heavy headed club an' the only club I ever saw him use that he never topped one with.

Conditions for shooting were none too good. It was as dark as a stack of black cats. The 13th green was twenty miles almost directly west of us. So I squared my dude around an' lined him up where he was shooting south to allow for that slice of his. I struck a match an' held it so my dude could take his stance an' make his practise swing. I knew I was taking a chance for if my dude overreached his ball like he sometimes did he would knock me off the butte.

My fat dude said he was ready. I lit another match an' held it as close as I dared. There was a crack like nobody's business an' the ball was on its way. It was impossible to follow the flight of the ball but it sounded good to me. My fat dude thought it was a good one too as he could feel it clear down to his toes.

At the crack of the ball Top Flite went scrambling down the butte. With my old soup houn' on the job there was nothing to worry about. The ball had crossed the river sure as it was a potent lick. But climbing down was really worse than when we had climbed the butte. It had me really worried. I didn't want to lose the very first dude I had started with an' have him killed this way.

An' my dude really enjoyed it. He told me so hisself. Onct we were back to the horses he said it was a "lark." It wasn't until the roar of the river hit his ears that he began to get full of panic.

I'll admit I lied a little then. It was the only out I had. I told my dude that shallow water playing over rocks was bound to be pretty noisy. The water was really shallow although it was a little swift. But as long as I knew this crossing like a book there was nothing for him to fear.

I started to tell him about some of the funny things that had happened when the outfit was rounding up. I started to tell him about the day Cat Claw had crossed right here. But I checked myself on this yarn when it occured to me

that it might not seem funny to him. As Cat Claw an' his pony came out a good half mile below.

The closer we came to the water the more the river roared. It was just as well my fat dude couldn't see what he was up against or I couldn't have got him in. But I yelled in his ear that I would lead his pony for him in case that he was nervous. I doubt if my fat dude heard me. If he did he didn't answer. Once we hit swimming water I knew he would be all right. By that time he would be too spooked to think of turning back.

Both horses knew the river. They had crossed it many times. It's places like this a pony always knows a heap more than a man who is riding him. When we hit the swimming water I turned his pony loose. If my dude tried to protest I didn't hear him.

There wasn't a bit of trouble from the time the horses waded in until they waded out the other side an' scrambled up the bank. Although we did come out a hundred yards below the place where I had figgered.

When I got off to pour the water from my boots my dude still sat his horse. He came through without a word. Not once did I hear a cheep from him after we started in. Considering it was strange to him that was something too.

It wasn't until I went to tell my dude how well he had done an' pat him on the back that I found he had been too spooked to even raise his voice. He was still too scared to speak.

(9)

DAY WAS BREAKING through the hills before my dude could speak. It wasn't until the first rays of the morning sun had touched Squaw Peak that he really found his voice. For a time it had me worried this silence of my dude's. I had read in a paper onct of a man who had been so badly scared he never spoke again. It was really a big relief to me to hear my fat dude's voice. In spite of the fact that onct he started in to talk I was afraid he would never stop.

Now that it was all over my dude enjoyed it too. To hear him talk the bear we had seen was really nothing now. But to have climbed Squaw Peak an' swam the river before daylight was something to talk about. Any one who ever told him of a sporty hole would hear about the 13th. There was only one fly in my fat dude's crock of milk. It made him feel prety low. It was the fact that no one would believe the yarn when he told about it later.

I had made a slip up, though, when I teed his ball that morning when we started. Allowing for my fat dude's slice I had him shooting south. It was really as much of a slip up on his part at that as any fault of mine. As he socked this ball just as straight as any ball that he had hit while he was in his daze.

The ball had carried the river though as there is quite a bend in there. That in itself was a break but if my dude had hit his ordinary slice as he had been supposed to do we would have cut off several miles.

But at that we won the thirteenth hole an' finished early too. Top Flite never lost a ball that day. He did some noble work an' the lesson I gave the cook an' wrangler at the 13th green was a mighty good one too as both of these birds were picked right clean before Balky got in that night.

With Balky an' his dude two down things looked mighty sweet until Balky had the nerve to pull our stunt an' cop a sneak next day. After his dude won the fourteenth hole we were only one up again.

It was nip an' tuck from there on in. It was anybody's match. The night we finished the 16th hole one down it looked pretty bad to me. Everything depended on the hole next day. It was really up to us. If we lost it the match was over then an' I was just a blowed up sucker.

An' the 17th was something to talk about, we battled all the way. Both dudes were neck an' neck that day until we reached the river. There was a right smart crowd all gathered there. They were ranged around the green. They gave our dudes a mighty cheer when our outfit hove in sight.

Both dudes cleared the river on their shots an' the crowd all cheered again. But it was nothing to the roar that followed when both dudes swung on their ponies an' headed for the river. Then the crowd all went hog-wild.

My dude I know was spooked that day. He told me so hisself. But he had already swum the river onct an' when I put it up to him that there was no other way back to the ranch he knew it was up to him.

But it was really my fat dude's pony who won the 17th. He was a swimming fool. He had scrambled out an' my fat dude was making his approach before the Chicago dude got over.

Dad had been sending riders out from time to time with balls for the dudes an' to find just where we were. That was the reason for all the crowd when we got into Golden Roll. Dad had come hisself to see the last hole played. An' such a crowd had gathered that two punchers had to kill another beef before they could all be fed.

Some reporters had got holt of the thing an' it had got into all the papers. Dad gave me one piece to read from the Arizona Republican. They played our match up big. They said that Arizona had the biggest an' sportiest golf courst in the world right here at the Bar X Ranch. They even gave the names of all the dudes an' where they were from who were playing on the courst.

They even went so far as to give a description of each hole. I guess Dad had never throwed off any when he gave the reporter this yarn. It said among other things that the shortest hole at Alkali was over thirty miles.

Dad said it was this yarn that got the two New York tabloids to send reporters out by plane. They started bidding as soon as we got in for the signed story of the first dude to finish the courst.

All the newsreel outfits on the coast had sent photographers too. They had been dickering with Dad an' he had been offered a pretty penny for the exclusive rights on the thing. But Dad had passed up this heavy dough. He said he would give them all a shot. That way it would be broadcast far an' wide. Dad figgered he would more than get his money back on the publicity he got for the courst.

Five cigarette outfits had representatives at the 17th green bidding for an endorsement of their brand. One of them wanted to blindfold every one in camp an' make some kind of test. This cigarette endorsement looks like a bad break for my dude in case he wins as he don't smoke. But when I mentioned same to them they said it made no difference.

There were hombres in camp who wanted their shaving soap endorsed. Tooth paste, talcum powder, socks an' shoes. In fact, every thing was represented. The winner was offered five hundred bucks just to say that he had drunk nothing but some kind of gingerale since he had been out on the courst. It looked to me as if the dude who won this thing was all set for the rest of his life.

There was plenty of betting too as to which dude would finish first. Because of the weight my dude had shed they made the odds against him. Take any man who has shed fifty pounds an' his clothes are bound to sag. But I know the shape my dude is in an' I take every bet that I can get when they offer two to one against him.

I bedded my dude early. It wasn't easy to do as with all the excitement about the camp he said he couldn't sleep. But I wanted him in A No. 1 shape for the 18th hole next day. An' my dude said he was feeling better than he had in twenty years. On the strength of this I went an' put my saddle an' bed roll up on him as I didn't have any more money. Yes sir, this match between the dudes had stirred up more excitement in these parts than anything that had happened since the Apache Kid was raiding.

The last hole going into the ranch is just about twenty miles, all of it slightly down grade. But in spite of the fact that the hole is down hill all of the way the hole has plenty of hazards.

The hole really follows Nine Mile Wash clear into the Headquarters ranch. It's not a hole where the lost ball problem is as big as on some other holes. As it's fairly open an' clear. But a man is shooting back an' forth across the sand wash on almost every shot.

There is a small box canyon on the 18th hole that calls for a mighty straight poke. The canyon is really wider than it looks but to the golfer who is facing it it resembles a needle's eye.

Once through the canyon the going is smooth except on the big sand wash. There are a couple of places where a man might cut off a mile or so by shooting through some short hills. But because of the cactus thickets that abound we knew it was foolish to try it.

As our dudes walked to the tee that morning to face the 18th hole they walked through a milling crowd. An attempt was made at order by some of the hands but people are worse than cattle. They milled an' churned about the dudes like long horns out of the brush.

The Chicago dude as a favorite had every thing his way. He had carried some extra rompers along which he put on that morning an' he had managed somehow to dig a razor up some place the night before an' get hisself shaved up.

I'll admit my dude didn't stack up so well when it come to how they looked. Because of the weight my dude had shed his clothes were all a bit loose. Some people in the crowd made wise cracks about the suspenders he wore. I'll admit the saddle strings didn't look like much but they were practical. But when one dude in the crowd went so far as to give my dude what is commonly called "the bird" I took a hand myself.

Dad was real decent about it too. He agreed that I was right. But he asked me as a favor to him not to shoot this dude until the match was over. But at least the crowd saw how things stood an' my dude got fair play. You could have heard a pin drop in the crowd as my dude addressed his ball.

But just because I'd pulled a gun my dude was all upset an' the clicking of the movie cameras as he went to shoot didn't really help him any. It was only natural that my dude should dub his drive.

When this Chicago dude lams one down the flat for a good two hundred with all the cameras clicking these birds who have bet their dough on him let out a yell. They think it's in the bag. When we have played about four miles an' the Chicago dude is so far out ahead of us he's almost out of sight these birds are sure of it.

When my dude an' I talked it over the night before I wanted to get him a faster horse. But my dude insisted that his cayuse was fast enough an' besides the pony knows him. But it looks to me as if he had made a big mistake the way every thing was going.

For Balky Bill had got his Chicago dude a fresh horse an' this pony is plenty fast. I know this pony pretty well. He's gentle just as long as things are going good. But just let one little thing go wrong an' I know he will spill the pack. As I watch him eating up the ground ahead of us I'm hoping something will happen.

They had played about eight miles, I'd say, an' the Chicago dude was still way out in front although he's not gaining any. My dude was pegging along like he always did an' since the crowd was following the Chicago dude my dude was doing better with his shots. He's hitting them just as far as he always did but I'm getting sicker all the time. His horse ain't fast enough.

I was just ready to kiss my saddle an' bed roll adios an' all my dough besides when I see a scatterment up ahead. An' I knew the thing that I've been hoping for has finally up an' happened. The Chicago dude has accidentally poked a niblick in his pony's flank an' his pony has bucked him off.

Aside from being jarred up some the Chicago dude aint hurt but this little incident throws him off his game an' he begins to dub his shots. An' since he is spooked of his pony now he takes plenty of time in mounting him an' plenty when he gets off.

There was plenty of water along the 18th hole where a man wouldn't suffer any. But I had carried a canteen along so 's to save all the time I could. But it was hard to get my dude held up even long enough to take a little drink.

I coached him along as best I could an' told him not to worry. An' if he would only think of his chin I'd tell him how things were going. But it wasn't until we reached the needle's eye that we caught the Chicago dude.

There is really a lot of head work to this game although it is seldom used. When my dude an' I talked the hole over the night before I told him about the needle's eye an' he agreed with me that he would use his putter there. I know with that old slice he had he could never make the grade.

That was where Balky an' the Chicago dude made their big mistake. His dude tried to use a brassie at first an' then he switched to a spoon. By the time he decided to use an iron the dude was so hot an' bothered he couldn't do any thing.

There was no telling how many shots he took, the balls flew thick an' fast. An' it didn't help the dude's feelings any when two of his backers were knocked completely cold by getting hit on the rebound. Balky got one in the ribs that just about knocked him off his horse. An' to make it real good the Chicago dude's pony got one in the flank that really upset him an' that old goat went to bucking again.

The Chicago dude was still firing when my dude an' I come up. When my dude used his putter an' put her through first lick I learned how fickle a crowd can be. The crowd all gave him a cheer. Balky's dude switched to his putter then an' put one through hisself an' as the dudes come down the home stretch it was anybody's match.

With the crowd all milling around us now my dude began dubbing again. All the talk I made about his chin didn't do a lick of good. Neither dude was even hitting far enough that he bothered to mount his horse.

With the 18th green not over a hundred yards away it was anybody's match. Both dudes were wet with sweat an' both dudes were swinging niblicks now for all that they were worth. One good shot by either dude was apt to reach the green.

When my dude pulled one into a cholla thicket I thought the jig was up. But right here was where my dude come through an' showed the stuff that he was made of. With his rear exposed to the cactus thorns he made the best niblick shot I'd seen in all them eighteen days. When his ball stopped rolling it was on the green not over three feet from the pin.

It wasn't until my dude come out of the thicket that we realized the punishment he had took. From the rear he resembled a porcupine when he stooped to address his putt.

Yes sir, it was that niblick shot that won the match. It almost lost it too. For between the cactus he had collected in his pants an' the clicking of the cameras about the green my dude don't make his putt. What's more he's further from the can on his second one than he was when he first started. But he finally got down in five putts an' everything was over. It was none too soon at that as the Chicago dude staggered onto the green just as my dude holed out.

(10)

THE RANCH DIDN'T LOOK much like the same old place when we got in that night. Dad had put in a service station an' garage to accommodate the dudes. He had put up another row of cabins too. Every one of them was full. As Balky an' I strolled about the place we felt almost like strangers.

The blacksmith shop was a "Pro Shop" now with Scotty MacDonald in charge. Scotty was too busy to even talk as he was just ready to give a lesson.

Dad had put in a "Sock 'em an' chase 'em" place on the flat that looked good to Balky an' me. But we couldn't even get clost enough to buy a few buckets of balls.

The runt courst in the calf corral was full of milling dudes. Old Tom, a crippled cowpuncher who used to tend the Cross S Ranch, was acting as starter there. Tom said it would be a good half hour before we could get on.

When we finally went inside to eat six flunkies were helping the cook. An' was that hombre on the peck? Cookie said he had been too busy to even swing a club all the time that we were gone. When he wanted Balky an' I to stick around until he was through we knew there was something up.

When we questioned the cook as to what the big idea was he said that Dad had put in lights at the calf corral so the dudes could play at night. An' while a few of the dudes were pretty good most of them were "fish." Cookie admitted then he had been putting some. As a matter of fact he finally said that picking dudes was the only thing he had to look forward to now that he couldn't play.

From Cookie we learned what had happened while Balky an' I were away. Dad had been putting on new cow hands every day just as fast as one rode in but it was quite a problem. The dudes had been coming in so fast it was hard to find enough cow hands to take them out on the courst.

Dad even tried sending out one cow hand with two dudes

but it didn't work out at all. This waddie lost both dudes before they had been out on the courst two days.

Some of the cow hands, not knowing the country, had been having trouble too. One waddie from New Mexico who had always worked on the flats got all balled up hisself. It had took his dude three days to finish No. 1.

Two dudes were reported lost in the steer trap on No. 4. There was another dude who had been lost two days according to Dolph, the packer. But Cookie didn't know for sure whether this dude was lost on No. 5 or if it was No. 7.

When I asked Cookie about the Cat Claw Kid he said he was out on the courst. The last time Old Dolph come in for a load of balls he had seen him on No. 6. I supposed he was still out with his long hitting dude until Cookie put me right. Come to find out this long hitting dude didn't finish No. 1.

When this long hitting dude ran out of balls he was ready to call it a day. He wanted to go back to the ranch. But knowing Dad's instructions Cat Claw told his dude that he wasn't really started and whether he liked it or not he was going to play the eighteen holes an' finish the courst before he went back to the ranch.

Naturally this dude protested but orders is orders to the Cat Claw Kid. An' that's what he told his dude. Personally, he said it would be all right with him if he never saw the dude again. But since he had his instructions he intended to follow them out. He told his dude to stay where he was while he went after more balls. That was when we met the Kid heading back for the ranch.

But this long hitting dude was a cagey dude who thought he was foxy too. He waited until the Kid was out of sight then he started back hisself. If the dude had followed the canyon back an' kept to the flats he would have made it too. But knowing he would meet the Cat Claw Kid he tried to cut off through the hills an' of courst he didn't go a mile before he got hisself plumb lost.

When Cat Claw got back with another peck of balls his dude was no place in sight. By cutting sign the Kid picked up his track. He hadn't followed it but a little piece until he guessed just what had happened. Cat Claw followed the track until almost dark when by luck he met the Swede.

Swede told the Kid if he would go to camp an' spend the night with him he would put his dogs on the dude's track next morning. It would be perfectly simple then. While his hounds had never hunted dudes Swede didn't think that tracking just one dude was apt to spoil his dogs.

Next morning when Swede showed old Pete the track the dogs all opened at onct. The dude had travelled some in the night but the dogs soon overtook him. Swede an' the Kid didn't follow the dogs ten miles until they heard them barking treed. But it wasn't so simple after all even after the dude was found. The dude had quit his horse an' climbed a tree. He was so scared of the dogs below him they couldn't coax him down.

It looked for a time as if the only way they could get the dude down was to shoot him out of the tree. But they finally compromised when the dude said if Swede would lead his dogs away he would come down of his own accord.

Cat Claw, of course, tried to get his dude to finish No. 1. But the long hitting dude was through. What's more he said that any time he lost a peck of balls he was through with golf for good. Yes sir, this long hitting dude was plumb burnt out as far as his golf game went.

"Shoot an' be damned" is exactly what he told the Kid. An' he told the Kid that he could even set the dogs on him again but he wouldn't play no more.

Orders is orders to the Cat Claw Kid. But that was where

Swede stepped in. Swede says as long as Cat Claw had never killed a dude it wouldn't look good to shoot the first one he had started with. He would explain it hisself to Dad. So Cat Claw took his long hitting dude on back to the ranch although he didn't want to do it.

The way Dad has put this thing acrost is hard to believe at times. The sale of golf balls alone runs into the serious money.

Of courst, it has its draw backs like any other business. Occasionally some dude comes in before he has finished the courst like this long hitting dude of the Cat Claw Kid's. But most dudes have too much pride to quit onct they have started out. Once in a while some dude's wife who is at the ranch makes such a fuss Dad has to send out on the courst an' have her dude brought in when he's only been out a week. Dad says there is never a day goes by but what it brings new problems.

Dad couldn't keep a cook at No. 3. None of them would stay because of the way the balls come off the hill when the dudes were approaching the green. Until Dad finally found a cook who had rode border patrol on the Rio Grande an' done a hitch in France. This cook used his head. He built hisself a dugout an' he takes to it when the dudes are approaching the green.

The wrangler who took to the brush an' quit the country the night our dudes came in has not been heard of since. There is always a man in most cow outfits whose conscience is none too clear.

Dad finally cleared this mystery up about the cook at Stinking Springs. We knew there was something queer the night that we camped there. Later the dudes began to gather there an' were perfectly satisfied to stay instead of moving on.

Dad knew it wasn't the water that was attracting every one. Of that much he was sure. An' come to find out this

cook had built hisself a still out in the brush an' was peddling hooch to the dudes.

As soon as Dad found the trouble he fired the cook right now. The idea of this cook having the nerve to pull such a stunt an' not offering to cut Dad in on it got Dad up in the air.

Dad solved the lost dude problem too although it took some time. Dudes still get lost occasionally. It's something that can't be helped. But after Dad put the Swede an' his dogs to work he rounds them up pretty fast.

A dude was just a dude to me when I started herding them. But I've learned that no particular town or state has a monopoly on the bad ones. I have herded several California dudes who hardly spoke at all. An' lately I had a New York

dude. If I had let my conscience guide me concerning him I would have knocked him in the head.

My fat dude from N. Y. came through an' sent me the new clubs just like he said he would. According to his note he's coming back an' play the courst again the first good chance he gets. He wants me to ride herd on him which I'll be glad to do. An' he wants to play the first nine holes again an' find out what they are really like when he is not unconscious.

An' speaking of dudes, Shorty told me a funny one about his Los Angeles dude. Shorty said that onct he got off the subject of California an' its climate he wasn't bad at all. But this funny thing I'm speaking of is what this dude told Shorty. In speaking of other things one day, just one thing an' another, this dude told Shorty casually that he had lived in California just two years an' that he was born in Iowa.

While herding dudes is harder work than herding stock there is more variety. It's really pleasant work. The only thing about the job that I don't like is the fact that I can't play. But just as soon as we can find two cow hands to take our place Dad has promised to let me an' Balky off to play the courst ourselves.

Scotty MacDonald is so busy now that Cookie helps him out. The cook is really Scotty's assistant yet he calls hisself a Pro. Cookie still wears rompers too but Buck an' Sears is out. Now Cookie has his rompers sent from Abercrombie and Fitch.

No sir, I wouldn't have believed this thing if I hadn't seen it happen myself. Because of the publicity about the courst Dad always has a waiting list. Now the dudes make reservations. Just the other day a golfer's magazine sent a reporter to the ranch. Dad was photographed in rompers while he gave his interview.

Some of the questions this bird shot at Dad were really hard to follow. Dad gave his cow hands credit too. He said that Balky an' Cat Claw really started things when they stole this sign in Phoenix.

But the reporter wasn't satisfied. He asked Dad how he came to think that he could put this thing acrost. It was the biggest golf courst in the world an' it was Dad's idea.

Dad's rompers were a little tight an' he unloosed the cinch to get a little air. It wasn't until he was comfortable again that he answered this bird's question.

"Any man," says Dad, "who follows the cow game all his life is more or less observing. It's a common trait with cow hands. But it's the man who observes the little things the average cow hand overlooks who always owns the outfit.

"Now I watched the dudes all pretty clost who dropped in here to play. While some of the fine points about the game were hazy to me there was one thing I always observed. It was mighty simple too.

"It was the fact that the tougher you made it for a dude an' the more misery he could deal hisself while he was on the courst the better he liked this game."